Team
ADVENTURE CLUB
COLD FRONT

Team ADVENTURE CLUB Cold Front

Joe Davison

4 Horsemen
Publications, Inc.

4 Horsemen
Publications, Inc.

4 Horsemen Publications, Inc.
1497 Main St. Suite 169
Dunedin, FL 34698
4horsemenpublications.com
info@4horsemenpublications.com

Cover by 4 Horsemen Publications, Inc.
Typesetting by Autumn Skye
Edited by SL Vargas

Library of Congress Control Number: 2021951206

Paperback ISBN-13: 978-1-64450-479-6
Audiobook ISBN-13: 978-1-64450-477-2
Ebook ISBN-13: 978-1-64450-478-9

DEDICATION

This book is dedicated to my daughters, Mia, Alexa, and Izabella. I long for the day that they too can lead a battle in space against a threat to humankind and have awesome gadgets and jet packs.

TABLE OF CONTENTS

PREFACE

Bellevue Heights is a sunny, seaside City that's warm in the afternoon and cool in the evenings. The long stretch of road that runs the length of the town is known as Seaside Drive. It starts some 15 miles at the exit off Interstate 45 and runs south for 25 miles. Along the way, you pass towns like Hawks Landing, Fishhook, Eagle Bay—the richest part of Bellevue Heights —and Tropical Estates, which is a series of beachside condos full of retirees ... and, finally, Bellevue Heights, established in 1935 by Orbert Schumacher, a German industrialist and railroad tycoon.

The city of Bellevue Heights was a small, quiet town until World War II. Then it became a booming destination for those who wanted to build a business, buy up land, and build real estate. It became a popular vacation destination when a millionaire opened up one of the largest water parks in all of America known as Tsunami Boom Boom, which is how Carrie Calusa's mother and father met back in 2000. When they were lifeguards in college.

Now, this redheaded 12-year-old is soaking up the sun and having the time of her life with her two best friends: Leanne McCallister, a dark-haired daredevil who loves to be upside down as much as right side up, and Robert Whitman, a skinny computer wizard and mechanic. These three can do it all. That's why, sometime last summer, Carrie came up with Team Adventure Club, dedicated to solving mysteries, finding lost animals, and discovering new, faraway places!

They are able to do this with the help of her amazing Uncle Max, a brilliant, and often strange, goofball. Uncle Max provides special equipment when needed, such as a laser gun or a toothbrush. Uncle Max's story is a long one. Once, he helped save the galaxy in an epic space battle when he was just 16 years old. Afterward, he had been sworn to secrecy by the government which left the family to believe that he made it all up. Only Team Adventure Club believes him.

Now, let's catch up with the amazing—and fantastically crazy—group of individuals known as Team Adventure Club!

CHAPTER 1

The day started off the same way it always did. Carrie and Leanne met on the steps in the front of the school while Robbie locked up their custom-made motorized scooters. Robbie's father, and Leanne's stepfather, was Mr. Whitman of Whitman Scooters, the number one rated motorized scooter company in the city. He donated Team Adventure Club three of the OHNO Z1 concept scooter, so they could get around the neighborhood faster. It also had the Whitman Scooter Logo down the neck of the scooter for advertising purposes. They were awesome. The scooters were silver in color, with big fat wheels and a pop-up seat if you wanted to sit instead of stand while riding. They had a huge headlight on the front and had been retrofitted with a USB plug for their wrist communication devices called TAC COM.

Robbie finished encoding his custom-designed touch screen lock and hustled his way over to the girls. He looked especially nice with his jeans and blue button-down shirt. Carrie started to smile at him but quickly frowned when she noticed his gaze was focused on Debra

Valentine, the school snob. Debra was the popular girl, the one with the fanciest clothes and shoes that money could buy. She walked like she was an English aristocrat, and every morning she arrived at school with an Iced Mocha Frabawhosawhatsit with extra whipped cream.

Carrie and Debra were old enemies. Debra ran the school like she was their queen, and Carrie was the smart kid who refused to bow down. Or the nerdy weirdo. Or the book worm. Or any of the other names Debra Valentine had called her.

Carrie's eyes narrowed as she watched Robbie smile and wave at Debra. Carrie looked at the mathematics book she was holding and politely placed it against the back of Robbie's head. With force.

Robbie staggered three steps down and looked back at Carrie in confusion. "What was that for?" he moaned.

"Why do you drool every time SHE walks by?" Carrie asked, pointing a finger.

"What? I don't... um... who?" Robbie tried playing it off as if he wasn't in love with Carrie's archnemesis.

"Robbie, you are gross sometimes," Leanne said with a snort. "C'mon, Carrie. We have to get to class." She grabbed the other girl by her arm and steered her toward the front entrance.

Robbie stood there watching them walk away rubbing his head. "I'm not going to get any smarter if you keep hitting me in the head!" he shouted.

"I was trying to pound some knowledge into your skull, dummy!" Carrie shot him a cheeky grin before heading inside.

Robbie rolled his eyes and followed the girls, and they all scattered to their respective classes.

Carrie found her seat in science class and put her science book on her desk. She loved science and learning how things worked. In fact, she liked most classes—except math. Numbers were the devil. But she managed to eke out a C+ in algebra, which brought her overall average down to a B, which she hated. Debra had a B average, too.

She pulled out her writing pad, which had T.A.C. printed on the top. She flipped it open, searching for her homework. Today was going to be a great day. They were going to dissect a rat. She was giddy with excitement.

Their teacher, Ms. Everborne, walked in pushing a huge cart. On it, were several metal trays each containing a large, dead rat. Carrie stretched up in her seat to get a better look. She smiled and looked back at her classmates, all of whom looked a little sick.

Ms. Everborne surveyed the classroom from her spot behind the desk. Her tall stature was intimidating to most students, but Carrie thought she was pretty. Her short hair was a shiny silver, and despite being what Carrie thought was possibly a hundred years old—again, not very good with numbers—she was a great teacher.

"Okay class, I'm breaking you into labs today. So, when I call your names, come up and get your rodent and supplies. Then we will get started," Ms. Everborne said with a huge smile.

Her energy barely contained, Carrie waited to find out who her partner would be.

"...next, Carrie Calusa and Debra Valentine, you are partners. Come get your rodent." Ms. Everborne smiled.

Carrie's heart shattered into a thousand pieces For a moment, her tongue got stuck to the roof of her mouth. Carrie and Debra's eyes met across the room. Caught in the crosshairs, Carrie imagined laser beams shooting at Debra as Debra also shot laser beams out of her eyes. The laser met in the middle of the classroom and the energy exploded causing all of their classmates' heads exploded in fiery balls of flame. Carrie leapt up, pulled a giant hammer out of thin air, and squished Debra flat. Then she calmly folded her up, stuck her in a large envelope, jumped out the window of the school and ran to the post office where, she mailed her to Talkeetna, Alaska.

"Ms. Calusa, come up here, please," Ms. Everborne said, pulling Carrie out of her fantasy.

"Coming!" Carrie said, faking a smile and sliding out of her seat. She joined her nemesis at the teacher's desk, trying to appear aloof.

Debra glared. "I don't like this anymore than you do!"

"I hardly doubt that," Carrie snapped back, making sure her fake smile was still firmly in place.

"Well bug brain, we should ace this thing since you're so smart and all." Debra sneered.

Carrie motioned toward the lab table. "Shall we?" Her smile turned a bit predatory.

Debra looked like she was trying to come up with a way to stuff Carrie into her own envelope.

Their mutual fantasy was cut short by Ms. Everborne. "You ladies play nice, or I'll make you permanent partners."

Both girls turned to look at their teacher with wide eyes, mouths falling open in twin looks of shock. But it did get them moving. They walked to one of the available tables topped with old scars and scratches from previous experiments gone wrong.

Carrie unrolled their instruments and laid out the cloth, setting everything up in a nice, neat line. Debra slammed the metal tray on the table, making everything jump—including the pickling liquid the rat was soaking in. It splattered on Debra's pretty dress. It smelled like old formaldehyde and shoe leather.

"Gross!" Debra squealed. She grabbed one of the brown paper towels sitting on the table and started scrubbing at her dress. No matter how hard she scrubbed, the smell didn't dissipate. With a small smile, Carrie watched her for a moment before picking up the rat to get a closer look.

Debra stopped scrubbing to gasp loudly. She stepped back from the table. "What is wrong with you, Carrie? That is so gross!"

"It's just a dead rat." Carrie rolled her eyes. "It's soaked in formaldehyde and is harmless. Besides, we're about to dissect it and find out if it's pregnant or not. This is science!"

Debra slowly stepped back to the table, looking like she wanted to be anywhere else but in class today. But since she didn't want Carrie Calusa to come out looking better than her, she swallowed hard and reached out, taking the rat from Carrie's hand. She could feel the cold wet fur sliding in her palm. She squeezed a little harder so that she didn't drop it and heard a crunch. The rat's sightless eyes seemed to be looking at her, judging her. Debra quickly put the rat back in the tray and forced herself to smile. "You're not so tough, Adventure Girl."

"Okay, Debra." Carrie packed as much sarcasm as she thought she could get away with into the words, mindful of their teacher's presence nearby. She really didn't want to get stuck with Debra for the rest of the year.

Carrie read the instructions Ms. Everborne had passed around and inserted one of the pins they had been given into each of the rat's feet. Now it looked like it was jumping in excitement. Then she picked up the scalpel and started to cut it open. Debra immediately closed her eyes and backed away.

"I can't, Ms. Everborne! This is too gross!" Debra screeched. The entire class looked at her. "I mean, it's not right. That animal deserves a peaceful rest, and here we are cutting it open."

Ms. Everborne looked up from her desk and stared for a moment. Then she smirked. She loved being right about her students; that's why she put her with Carrie. She knew Debra would have a hard time with this assignment. "Ms.

Valentine, get back to your table and help Ms. Calusa with the project, or I will flunk you both."

"Ms. Everborne, this is so gross," she complained. Debra looked back at Carrie and the rat.

"It's not gross; it's science." Ms. Everborne got up and came to their table. "Here, I'll help." She pulled up a stool and sat down, taking the scalpel from Carrie.

"Ms. Everborne, I can do this just fine," Carrie whined.

"Of course you can, but you can't do everything yourself. One day, you'll find something you can't do, and you'll need to ask someone for help. Learning to work as a team is as important as learning to do things independently." Ms. Everborne gave her a warm smile.

Carrie sighed and nodded, stepping back to watch. "Okay class, everyone gather around this table, and I'll explain everything as I go." With that, Ms. Everborne started dissecting the rat.

There was a low "ewwww" that fell across the classroom, but Carrie just smiled.

CHAPTER 2

Sitting in his history class, Robbie took notes with glee. He loved history, especially American History. The West. The Civil War. The Steam Age. He loved it all. His teacher, Mr. Polsty, had the perfect history teacher look: a full beard with no hair on his head, pants stained with yellow chalk around the pockets, and a brown corduroy jacket that had elbow patches.

Robbie wanted desperately to own a jacket just like that. He looked them up on eBay once, but they cost far more than he could scrape up in allowance money. He also admired that Mr. Polsty smoked a pipe outside during his lunch break. Even though smoking was disgusting, it made him look like either Leonardo Da Vinci or a steamboat captain. Robbie wanted to be just like him when he got old.

"That is why Lewis, Clark, and their Native American guides were able to mark the majority of the locations on today's maps. Can you imagine traveling the countryside with your best friend? One of you on land, the other on the river in a canoe. Your trusty dog at your side."

While Mr. Polsty continued talking about Lewis and Clark, Robbie slipped into his own world for a moment. He thought about Team Adventure Club exploring unknown planets, conquering monsters, and fighting pirates on the seven seas. He quickly snapped out of it when Mr. Polsty called his name. "Well, Mr. Whitman?"

Embarrassed, Robbie stared at the man he admired. "Ummm, what is Montana?" Robbie hazarded a guess based on a quick glance at his notes.

"Indeed!" Mr. Polsty said with a hearty gesture.

With a weak smile, Robbie sank back into his seat, wiping his brow. A chubby boy wearing cargo shorts and a striped button-down shirt leaned over to whisper to him. "That was quick! Were you thinking about Debra Valentine again?" he asked with a smile and a wink.

The boy was Malcolm Donaldson, Robbie's friend. The only reason he wasn't part of Team Adventure Club with the rest of them was because his parents didn't allow him to stay out past 7:30 on school nights and 8:30 on the weekends. His family always went away on trips over the summer, which is when Team Adventure Club had most of their adventures.

Robbie shook his head. Malcolm thought otherwise. He knew Robbie was fascinated by Debra, and he constantly teased him about it. As the bell rang, Robbie and Malcolm headed to their next class together: gym. Malcolm hated gym class. He couldn't run. He couldn't climb rope. He couldn't play volleyball, basketball, or baseball. He could punch the punching bag, so that's what he did for the entire class. Robbie, however, was head of the class. Malcolm might count the minutes until the bell rang, but for Robbie, it was never long enough. He loved to climb rope, swim, and run. Robbie wasn't satisfied just punching the bag, though he would take turns with Malcolm just to keep his friend company.

Coach Twinkle was a large man; he was tall and wide with bulging muscles and a thick mustache. His nose was pointed downward, and his hair was buzzed short. Most students feared him, and Robbie was no exception. "Robert Whitman! Eight minutes and ten seconds on the mile, boy! Pick up the pace. And tell your chubby little friend that walking doesn't count as running!" Coach Twinkle's voice bellowed like a bull horn.

Robbie waited for Malcolm as he slowly walked over the finish line. Just as he was about to say good job to his friend, Coach Twinkle stepped in, overshadowing Malcolm like the sun eclipsing the moon.

"Donaldson! By the end of this year, I'm gonna have you running like your friend here. I know it's tough being overweight. I was there once, too, little fella. I was a fat chocoholic. I ate candy and sugar all day. Then one day I saw a war movie. I knew that life was for me. I wanted to be a soldier fighting the good fight! From that moment on, I worked hard at becoming a heavyweight, not an overweight. Say it with me! A heavyweight, not an overweight!"

"A heavy-weight, not an overweight," Malcolm sighed.

"Good. Now hit the showers. You smell like a cheeseburger!" Coach Twinkle smacked Malcolm on the back with enough force to push him a few feet forward.

Robbie and Malcolm took the opportunity to run while they still could. Back in the locker room, they sat on the bench, catching their breath. Malcolm was slumped over and tired, while Robbie got busy changing back into his school shirt.

"So, are you going to come over this weekend and finally join Team Adventure Club?" Robbie's voice was muffled as he pulled his shirt over his head.

"I want to, but my parents want to go to our grandparents for dinner on Sunday. So, probably not. I'll never get to be a member of the club!" Malcolm sighed.

"That's not true! I can make you an honorary member. You can be an outside advisor for the club. If there's ever any cases we can't solve, we'll come to you." Robbie popped his head out of his shirt's neck hole, his hair sticking up.

"Really?! Do you mean it?" Malcolm's face lit up.

"Yes, of course I mean it," Robbie said. "C'mon, we have to get to math class. I have Carrie's homework."

"Is she still having trouble in math?" Malcolm asked.

"Isn't she always?" Robbie said, smacking his friend on the shoulder as they walked out of the locker room and into the busy hallway.

CHAPTER 3

Carrie fidgeted in her seat, trying to be patient as she waited for Robbie. She really liked him, but Robbie was too dumb to realize it. He was too busy being obsessed with Debra Valentine. Carrie couldn't understand how someone like Robbie could have such a huge crush on a mean girl like her. She wondered what Debra had that she didn't.

When Robbie finally walked into class, she sighed. He was handsome, well-groomed, and stylish. She looked down at herself. She wasn't stylish at all: her pants were well worn, as were the favorite pair of hiking boots she always wore. Her canvas satchel was held together with duct tape on one of the corners, and other parts had been stitched and re-stitched a million times.

"Hello, Carrie! You okay?"

She jumped, realizing Robbie was now standing over her desk. "What? Oh, I must have been daydreaming."

"Here's your homework. I got questions seven and ten wrong on purpose. You're not very good at math, remember?" Robbie grinned.

"Yeah, thanks a million, Robbie." Carrie tried to fight back the wave of sadness. Maybe that was why he didn't like her. Maybe she was a little too stupid at math. *Is Debra smarter at math?*

"Carrie, are you even listening to me?" Robbie poked her arm.

"What?" Carrie blinked at him a few times, trying to get her brain back on track.

"Never mind. We have a meeting at 8:30 tonight at the treehouse. Don't forget," Robbie said.

"The treehouse is in my backyard. How am I going to forget?" She mustered up a smirk.

"Yeah right!" Robbie rolled his eyes and made his way over to his seat just as their teacher walked in.

"Okay class, take your seats and let's get that homework turned in," Mr. Falvo said. He was a short Japanese man with a bow tie. He had a different one every single day, coordinated by color. Monday: blue; Tuesday: yellow; Wednesday: red; Thursday: green; and Friday: he chose any color he wanted.

He was a genius and had won many international awards for his theories in mathematics. He didn't like when students didn't understand. He felt that everyone should have an easy understanding of all numbers. Carrie, though, didn't like math. She would rather be in science, history, or reading up on paleontology. Math was just so hard. Thank goodness for computers, calculators, and Robbie.

Mr. Falvo walked down the aisle collecting everyone's homework. When he reached Carrie's desk, he examined her paper slowly, squinting his eyes. "It is quite amazing how much your sevens look just like Robbie Whitman's sevens. Don't you think so, Miss Calusa?"

Carrie gave her teacher a wide grin, hoping to come off as innocent. "Uh, I guess?"

"Not a guess. Fact. I'm on to you two. That is why I have assigned a special project for you alone, Miss Calusa." Mr. Falvo's tight lipped smile looked like a demonic beaver, and this made Carrie shiver.

He pulled a bag from out of nowhere. Inside was a legal sized yellow paper tablet of paper and workbook with perforated worksheets inside. Mr. Falvo handed Carrie the workbook as he slowly bowed to her. "This is a study book on basic algebra. You will complete one page per night. There are two-hundred and forty-seven pages inside. That is two hundred and forty-seven nights of studying simple mathematics. See what I did there?" As Carrie felt her eyes beginning to water against their will, her teacher's face softened slightly. "I want you to learn Miss Calusa. I'm not here to try and trick you into failing. Everyone deserves the chance to succeed. This workbook will help you learn to understand numbers. I'm no different than you. For me, it's spelling. I can solve a quantum equation in a snap but ask me to spell 'liverwurst' or 'parameterization,' and I'm at a loss. I must spend extra time learning the composition of words so that I can succeed. Do the workbook, and you will succeed with numbers. The key is to learn to enjoy it. I know you have an A in history, and that is because you love history. Figure out how to love math, and you will find yourself just as successful here."

Carrie sighed and nodded. She knew Mr. Falvo meant well. And he was right: his spelling was atrocious. She had heard some of the other teachers talking at last week's Pep-Rally about how they could barely make out his post-it notes in the teachers' lounge.

She thumbed through the workbook, looking at the little drawings of kids smiling and having a blast doing math. *Kids don't actually jump up and down while doing math*, she thought. Then she noticed Andre Riessig, a German exchange student, actually jumping up and down by the chalkboard as he solved the weekly question.

"Weeeeeeeee!" He shouted just like a kid who had just won a toy at the fair.

Carrie shook her head. She looked over at Robbie and found him staring at her. "What?" she asked.

"You could have gotten us both in trouble," Robbie whispered.

"Why didn't you make my numbers look different than yours?" she whispered back.

"Oh, I'm sorry for doing your homework every day!" He grabbed her pencil and threw it to the back of the room. In retaliation, she smacked the back of his head.

Robbie reached back and grabbed the back of her left knee, tickling her. Carrie squirmed in her chair trying not to make a sound, but it was no use. She let out a squeak that sounded like a bird had flown into the room. Mr. Falvo looked around to see where the noise had come from.

"Miss Calusa. Would you like to share something with the class?" He raised an eyebrow at her.

"No, Mr. Falvo. I had to sneeze." She rubbed her nose dramatically.

He squinted at her. "Oh, well then. Bless you."

"Thank you." Carrie hid her face and kicked the back of Robbie's chair.

Mr. Falvo returned to the chalkboard and drew several shapes. "My three favorite shapes: the square, the trapezoid, and the parallelogram. Can anyone tell me how to find the dimensions of each?" He scanned the sea of raised hands until he found Carrie, her arms firmly folded.

"Ah, Miss Calusa. Come up to the board." He held out a piece of chalk.

Carrie looked helplessly at Robbie, her eyes wide. After a moment, he reached into his bag. He always carried around a ton of gadgets that he was tinkering with for Team Adventure Club. This time, he pulled out a pair of eyeglasses.

"Carrie? Don't forget your glasses." He handed them to her.

She cocked her head at him. "I don't wear glasses," she whispered.

"Just put them on. Trust me."

Carrie did as he asked, blinking when the room turned a dull purple color through the lenses. She pulled glasses down again, and the room returned to its fluorescent glory. She put the glasses back on: still purple. Turning back toward the chalkboard, she saw the same drawings waiting for her, and she sighed. Deep down, she had hoped Robbie's invention were magical multiplying math mastering magnifiers, but no such luck.

At the chalkboard, she picked the square. As she started to trace it, the glasses activated. To her delight, it traced the square along with her, measuring each side. The equation appeared: C = d x 0.14645, D = s x 1.14142 = 1.414 4/A, S = Dx0.7071 = /A, Area A – S(2) = ½ D(2), then she drew a circle with a square in it putting a D in the center of the square a C on the outside of the circle and a S on the outside of the Square. Carrie wrote the equation on the chalkboard, trying to hide her excitement. She wanted to jump for joy like Andre Reissing had.

Mr. Falvo gave her a long look before nodding. "Very good, Miss Calusa. You may have a seat."

As Carrie looked at him, the glasses started measuring every inch of his body, calculating his dimensions and proportions. Wherever she looked, the glasses did the same calculations: the stapler, the back wall, the pencil on her desk, Sally Johnson's face, the zit on Sally Johnson's face. The numbers kept coming, piercing her eyes like pins and needles. She felt dizzy. She leaned on Mr. Falvo's desk, but when she looked down at her hand on the desktop, it measured that too. She couldn't take it anymore. She couldn't see straight. As the darkness approached, she dimly heard Robbie and Mr. Falvo calling her name. She grabbed the side of her head.

"My head," she moaned.

As she looked at Robbie for help, the glasses slid off her face as she hit the ground.

Everything went dark.

Carrie returned to awareness slowly. When she opened her eyes, the light felt blinding and overwhelming, so she quickly closed them again. She felt around keeping her eyes closed. She could feel the coarseness of the blanket on top of her and the sticky pleather cushion under her back and realized she was in the nurse's office. Sitting up begrudgingly, she kept her eyes firmly closed. She could still see the remnants of fractions and equations burned into her eyelids.

Rubbing her eyes, she felt the headache slam back into her brain. She laid back down again, not wanting to puke, but it was a lost cause. Just as Robbie walked through the door, everything she had in her stomach came flying out, soaking his shirtfront. Robbie tried to escape but slammed into the door and slipped in Carrie's sick. He landed in a heap on the floor.

"Robbie?" Carrie called in a weak voice.

"Yes?" Robbie's voice wavered.

"Did I just puke on you?"

"Yes. Per usual."

Carrie just sighed. She had puked on him more than once.

Nurse Habberdash came into the room armed with paper towels, which she gave to Robbie. He promptly started smearing the puke off his jeans. "Robbie, you might want to change your clothes, sweetie," the nurse said.

He gave her a "duh" look behind her back, then waddled off to the nearby bathroom.

"Carrie, I called your parents. Your mother is on her way to pick you up," Nurse Habberdash said. "Have you ever had a migraine before?"

"No, ma'am," Carrie said.

"Well, just lay there until your mother gets here, okay?" The nurse set about cleaning up the puke.

Meanwhile, in the bathroom, Robbie was as clean as he could get. Since he didn't regularly come to school with a change of clothes, he was stuck wearing what he had on. He smelled terrible. He looked in the mirror and saw that he had puke in his hair, so he washed his scalp with hand soap as well.

He stepped out of the bathroom just in time to see Carrie's mom, Sandra Calusa, walking away with a miserable Carrie. Sandra Calusa was a tall woman, and she sported the same red hair Carrie had inherited. Robbie thought she looked like someone from the 1950's with the way she dressed, but he knew she was only in her thirties. She was pretty. He knew that for sure.

"Mrs. Calusa!" Robbie yelled as he ran down the hallway to catch up to them.

Turning, Mrs. Calusa blinked. "Robbie, why are you all wet?"

Carrie turned, her eyes still tightly closed. "I puked on him," she whispered.

"Oh my. Robbie, dear, come with us. I'll take you home. You can't spend the rest of the day at school like that." She pulled out her cell phone, already starting to dial. "I'll call your mother and let her know. Take Carrie to the car, and I'll check you out."

As she walked away, already chatting with his mom, Robbie helped Carrie out the door and put her in the front seat of the car. He rummaged through his bag of "unusual items" as he called it until he found a sleep mask. He slipped it carefully over Carrie's eyes. "I'm really sorry, Carrie. I didn't realize they would make you so sick."

"It's okay, Robbie. I'm never cheating again. Not if it causes this much of a headache. Besides, it was cool for about thirty seconds. I see potential for the glasses. Once you work out the bugs," she replied softly.

Robbie got in the back seat then snapped his fingers. "Our scooters!" He jumped back out again just as Mrs. Calusa walked up.

"Where are you going, Robbie? I'm responsible for you!"

"Yes, Mrs. Calusa, I know. But our scooters are here. I'll drive Carrie's home, then you can bring me back to get mine." He started running toward the bike rack.

"Fine! You've got twenty minutes, and I want you to call me at every corner." She got into the car, giving him a firm look.

Robbie watched the car pull away before pulling a small monitor out of his bag, connecting it to the scooter. He put his cell phone on its clip and a Bluetooth headset in his ear. Then, he flicked a switch and a light started blinking on the scooter's console. Ready, he started for Carrie's house.

Inside the car, something started beeping. Mrs. Calusa looked around for the source of the noise.

"Mom, hit the red switch on the radio," Carrie mumbled, already half-asleep. Mrs. Calusa pushed the button, and immediately, Robbie started talking.

"Mrs. Calusa, this is Robbie. I've connected to your Blue Tooth through our TAC COM's."

"Oh, that's lovely," Mrs. Calusa said, keeping her eyes on the road.

"Also you'll see a red dot on your GPS monitor, and you can track the scooters. Any time the scooters are active, you can locate them on any GPS compatible device!" Robbie shouted.

"Okay!" Mrs. Calusa shouted back.

"Mother!" Carrie cried out, slapping her hands over her ears in an attempt to keep her brain from leaking out.

"Oh, I'm sorry dear. Robbie was shouting so I thought maybe I needed to as well." Mrs. Calusa lowered her voice to a whisper.

"Okay, bye!" Robbie shouted.

"Bye, Robbie!" Mrs. Calusa shouted back again. "Sorry again, dear."

Carrie just moaned.

Robbie jetted down the sidewalk and was quickly on the bay side of the city. He could feel the salty ocean air on his skin, which did nothing to drown out the fresh smell of vomit on his clothes. He tried not to breathe, but he could only hold his breath for so long. He called to check in with Carrie's mom, giving her an update on his progress.

At the house, Carrie's mom helped her inside and up the stairs to lie down in her own bed. As Mrs. Calusa waited for Robbie to arrive, she checked the mail, putting a small box addressed to Carrie on the table by the front door. Then, she started puttering around the kitchen, pulling out what she would need for dinner later. As she waited, her husband, Theodore Calusa, walked in, home a bit early from work.

"Well, hello to the most wonderful woman in the world!" He moved in for a kiss only to be thwarted by Mrs. Calusa's inattention. She was still thinking about dinner.

"There's chicken and sides for dinner tonight. I preheated the oven. Can you be a dear and get that started for me?" she asked.

Mr. Calusa just stood there with his lips puckered, making kissy noises.

"I have to take Robbie back to school to get his scooter. Carrie puked all over him today," she added.

"Again?" Mr. Calusa laughed.

She looked up and finally noticed his puckered lips. She gave him a small kiss and a smile before heading to the master bedroom to change out of her suit.

Mr. Calusa squinted, and his eyebrows knit together. "Why did she puke on him?"

"No idea. She got a bad headache and vomited, the nurse said," she called back.

"Is she okay?" Mr. Calusa followed her into the bedroom, concerned.

Mrs. Calusa slide a large comfy hoodie over her head, destroying her perfect hair as it morphed into what look like a bird's nest instantaneously. She scratched her stomach and yawned widely.

Mr. Calusa did a double take looking at his wife.

"She said she's fine but wanted to lay down."

"Who are you and what have you done with my wife?

Mr. Calusa headed up the stairs to his daughter's room. "Carrie? Sweetie? You okay?"

Carrie rolled over on her bed to face the door. "Yeah. I'm fine, Dad. My head just hurts a lot."

"What happened?" Mr. Calusa sat down on the edge of her bed, careful not to jostle her. Around the black sleeping mask, his daughter's face was olive green with a slight hint of yellow. Mrs. Calusa caressed Carrie's hair, putting it around her left ear.

"I don't know. I was wearing these glasses Robbie made, and they made me sick."

"Oh gosh, sweetie, I'm sorry. Do you want something for the pain?" he asked.

"Mom gave me medicine already. I'll be fine. I have a club meeting tonight, so I have to rest."

"Maybe you should skip the meeting tonight," Mr. Calusa said gently.

Carrie snapped the sleeping mask up onto her forehead, looking at her dad through bloodshot eyes. She scanned her father's head as if she was still wearing the glasses, but there were no measurements to be seen. "I've never missed a meeting, and it's not happening tonight."

"They can have the meeting without you."

"Dad! It's in our backyard, in the treehouse, just like every Wednesday. We have to get ready for this weekend. We have to find Mrs. Keller's dog Pogo, remember?" Carrie said.

"Well, you've got a few hours until then. Take a nap." He brushed the rest of her hair out of her face.

"Okay, dad. Love you." Carrie pulled the mask back down over her eyes, laying her head back on the pillow.

As Mr. Calusa came down the stairs, Robbie came through the front door, still in his wet clothes. "So, what happened today at school? Carrie told me you made some glasses?"

"Oh, well, yeah. See, I took this old glass plate from a calculator, integrated it with a microchip, and then added in an instant size algorithm. When you look at things, it measures them and runs calculations. You can do things like calculate the distance from one side of a cavern to the other in case you have to jump or something. Well, Carrie put them on, and it made her sick." Robbie shook his head, feeling guilty about hurting her so badly.

"They still need to be balanced for what and when to measure, I guess," Mr. Calusa said.

"Sure." Robbie assumed Carrie's father didn't really understand the mechanics of the glasses, so he didn't bother to try and explain further.

"Are you ready, Robbie?" Mrs. Calusa popped her head into the room, keys in hand.

Robbie was more than ready to get his own scooter so he could go home and change into dry, non-smelly clothes. He nodded enthusiastically.

"Let's go then. Dear, I put everything in the oven for dinner. Just keep an eye on it for me. We'll be back in about twenty minutes. Set the table for five—remember it's Wednesday, so the rest of the club will be here at eight. Don't even try to ask if she's going to miss it." She paused, counting on her fingers for a moment. "Actually, set it for six. If I know Max, he'll be here, too."

Carrie laid in bed listening to a local news show on an old 1970s brown and yellow radio she had bought at a garage sale last summer. The left dial was missing, but that didn't matter since she fixed it with a small pair of needle nose pliers. There was white backing from old stickers that had long since been ripped off and the only sticker left was a sticker of a puppy from a long-lost cartoon she barely remembers. But she loved her radio. After all, she spent days tinkering on it and getting back into working condition. Been working for over a year now. Unfortunately, it only got two stations: one that featured a local talk radio show and a second that played a syndicated horror mystery show at 2am. She listened to the news, letting her brain rest after the overload this afternoon, when a news bulletin caught her attention.

"This just in. It appears there is a comet that is going to be flying within the Earth's atmosphere just over Bay Side Beach at 11:15 tonight. Scientists speculate that this is a random comet, and there should be no cause for alarm. It is expected to crash into the ocean, having little effect on anyone or anything. But if you're out at the beach and want to watch something spectacular, this should do it."

CHAPTER 4

Leanne, oblivious to the trials of her friends, listened to Ms. Yoder explain the universe. She loved science class. It was her best subject besides math, history, and biology. Except, sitting two rows from her was Debra Valentine. Leanne wasn't a fan of Debra because Debra used her looks to manipulate other students into liking her. She was mean to other students who didn't have a much money as her and talked down to them. However, Debra's face was flawless, and she was so pretty. Leanne did admire her for that. She was stunning but that didn't give her the right to hurt people less fortunate. Leanne was one of the few students who had stood up against Debra.

Distracted, Leanne started thinking about flying. That was her stress relief. She loved flying her father's plane. Leanne had been taking flying lessons for two years now; her father owned MaCalister Airfield and gave lessons for a living, so when Leanne turned ten, he started teaching her how to pilot small aircraft.

She could fly a plane on her now. Once, she flew her and her dad to the next state to get her mom's favorite dessert, the Super Chunky Chocolate Choco Mocha Lava Cake from Big Bob's Dessert Den. Mrs. MaCalister still thought Mr. MaCalister went alone. The memory made Leanne smile, but reminiscing also made her lose track of the lecture.

Now I want chocolate, Leanne thought.

Leanne didn't realize she was still staring at Debra until the other girl caught her. "What are you staring at?" she quietly hissed.

"What?" Leanne snapped out of her daydream.

"You were staring at me. Weirdo!"

"I was daydreaming. I'm sorry," Leanne apologized.

"Well, maybe you should go see if your girl-friend is okay instead," Debra snapped.

Leanne blinked. "What are you talking about?"

"Oh, you didn't hear that Ms. Adventure herself got sick in math class and threw up all over the nurse's station and Robbie Whitman?" Debra looked down her nose at her as she talked.

"When?"

"Like ten minutes ago." Debra turned her cell phone so Leanne could see a video of Carrie passing out. "I'm going to put this up on my blog."

"You'd better not, Valentine!" Leanne shook her fist at the other girl.

"Or what?" Debra's eyes narrowed dangerously.

"Excuse me. Would you two young ladies prefer to be the ones teaching this class?" Ms. Yoder asked.

Both girls turned back to the front of the room, shaking their heads. Ms. Yoder was an older woman, about fifty or so. Her hair was a wavy mess of salt and pepper color, and she believed that most children needed more homework. She was strange, but a good teacher, nonetheless. "Well, good! I would like to continue the lesson, if that's okay with both of you?"

"Sorry," Leanne mumbled.

"Sorry," Debra muttered.

"Good. Now if you girls would come up here, I want to demonstrate mass quantum gravitational polarity in the universe," Ms. Yoder said.

Leanne and Debra made their way to the front of the class, both still embarrassed. Debra recovered more quickly, waving as if she was in a parade and giving a curtsy to her classmates. She flipped her hair and smiled wide. The boys cheered, and Debra's friends clapped. She winked.

Leanne just shook her head. Unimpressed, she looked out over the class. Most only flattered Debra so she wouldn't single them out and make fun of them in the hallways. They knew that if you kept your mouth shut and clapped as Debra Valentine walked by, she would leave you alone. Leanne wasn't afraid of Debra. She'd flown a plane through a thunderstorm at night, and after that most things seemed small potatoes compared to lightning hitting your plane.

The lesson continued, and when the bell finally rang, Leanne had never been happier to get out of that class. She grabbed her bag and ran out of the classroom, pulling out her official T.A.C. Communication wrist-radio to call

Carrie. "Carrie, what happened in math class? Are you okay?"

Since students weren't allowed to use cell phones unless it was an emergency, Uncle Max had created the devices for the club. They resembled a watch, but they had a large face and a camera so that they could video chat, record images, and take pictures. They called them TAC COM, and they were awesome, to say the least.

"Leanne, hey." Carrie's image appeared on the watch face, and Leanne could tell she was in bed. She wore a sleep mask over her eyes and made no move to remove it.

"What happened?" Leanne repeated.

"It was awful! Robbie made these calculating glasses, but all the numbers hurt my brain."

"Do you still want to have the club meeting tonight?" Leanne asked.

"Yes! I will never miss a meeting, Leanne! What's oath number three?"

Leanne was impressed she could tell that Carrie was glaring at her through her sleep mask.

"Members never miss a Team Adventure Club meeting, no matter what!" Leanne raised her right hand, much like they had when taking the oath. "I was just checking, grumpy!"

"I know. I'm sorry. My head hurts."

"Okay. I'll be there in a few hours. Where's Robbie?" Leanne asked.

"I think he's home or coming back here. I'm not sure," Carrie answered.

"Just get some rest and I'll be there shortly. Leanne, over and out!"

Leanne touched the screen, and a small map appeared. Robbie's red dot was moving quickly through the streets, so she knew he had to be on his scooter. She quickly touched the screen again to call him.

"Did you talk to Carrie?" Robbie shouted over the noise of his scooter.

"Yeah. What did you do to her?" Leanna asked. She hustled through the halls to her next class.

"I didn't mean to. The glasses started malfunctioning. I have to take them to Uncle Max. He can fix them."

"I'm going home to change. Carrie puked all over me," Robbie explained.

"You probably deserved it!" The bell rang loudly; she was going to be late for class if she didn't hurry.

"Call me later. Get to class before you get a referral."

"Okay. I'll see you guys in a bit." She flipped her TAC COM off and opened the door to her next class. The art studio was dark and empty. She smacked her forehead, suddenly remembering that class was outside today.

Leanne rushed to the window, looking down two stories to the field where the rest of the class had gathered. There was a quicker way to get down there. She pulled a small device with a hook and a cable out of her bag and aimed it at a large oak tree several yards away. She fired and attached the other end of the cable to the window ledge to create a zipline.

Mrs. Brunswick was talking to a student and wasn't looking in her direction. Perfect timing. Leanne slid down the cable, hit the release, and dropped down by the oak tree. She quickly joined the rest of the class on the grass, slinging her backpack off and leaning back against it like she had been there forever. Several students looked at her in amazement.

One, in particular, Yogi Zibberaluga was very impressed.

"Ah, krasavitsa, you are but daring. You and I should be together, no?"

Leanne smiled at him. The foreign exchange student's dark hair was tied back in a ponytail, giving him an exotic look and his accent was cute. She blushed a little. "Well, maybe."

Mrs. Brunswick did a double take when she noticed Leanne. "Oh, good. We're all here. But Miss MaCalister, shouldn't you be in Economics class? You have art sixth period. This is fifth period, sweetie."

Leanne looked around and realized she didn't really know any of the kids in the class except Yogi, who was in her gym class. She groaned. *What a day.*

CHAPTER 5

The large tower cast shadows on the other buildings downtown. Its huge glass roof reflected sunbeams like a satellite bouncing signals. There wasn't a spot in the city where you couldn't see the tower. "The eyesore of the city," some people called it. "The Hedgestone Tower of Doom," said others. Either way, it was owned by billionaire Sir Oliver Hedgestone. He was an older man, short, with a slick, bald head. He was ruthless and mean and had no heirs for his fortune. He was married for a time, but his wife—Susan Elizabeth Marybeth Hedgestone—died of cancer years ago, and he never married again.

The hallways on the top floor were made of marble. The clacking of his expensive shoes rapped on the floor as he walked, six of his assistants hurrying to keep up with his long strides. Sir Oliver Hedgestone never had less than three assistants with him at all times.

A set of large double doors opened, and he made his way into his office. The entire office could see out over Bayside Beach, the neighborhood of Bellevue Heights, and the entire city. He stepped onto a small mat, and one of his assistants knelt down and took off his right shoe followed by the left, then slipped his feet into a pair of yellow Crocs.

Hedgestone continued to his large Cherry Oak desk, sitting down in his oversized leather chair. It wasn't typical leather, but rather buffalo leather, with a large, stuffed buffalo head mounted to the chairback. Hedgestone looked down and noticed that his solid gold pen was crooked, so he straightened it, ensuring everything was perfect. "Well?" he said, looking up at his assistants.

The six fumbled nervously, pulling out notes and paperwork. The first to speak was Jenny Venola, who had been with Sir Oliver Hedgestone the longest. "I have your stock market ratings. We're up thirty-two percent for today, sir. It seems that endeavor with World Wide Global is paying off. We fired eighteen people at Hedgestone Coffee, twenty-six people at Hedgestone Power, and we are moving to a completely robotic assembly line at Hedgestone Motors and should see the entire staff of four hundred and eighty released by next Friday. I had the Human Resources department propose a severance package which needs your approval. You have a meeting with the governor at 12 p.m. to discuss the recent merger of Hedgestone Nuclear and Bellevue Power." She laid a folder on his desk.

Hedgestone opened a wooden box by pressing a series of numbers on the lid's keypad. It opened to reveal dark-rimmed glasses, which he slid on before reaching for the folder. He looked at the severance proposal for a moment before leaning back in his chair. "Does this seem reasonable to you, Ms. Venola?" he asked.

"Yes. These people will have to feed their families while they look for another job." She adjusted her glasses.

"How long does it take to find a job?"

"It varies, but perhaps three months or longer, sir," she replied.

"Proof?"

She held out her hand, and another assistant handed her a piece of paper. "According to the Job and Securities Regulation Association, it takes an average person of high school education three to six months to find a well-paying job. In certain technical vocations, it could take up to six months."

"Fine. To think of children," Hedgestone said with a condescending tone.

She picked the folder back up and nodded. She nodded, then waved the assistants out of the office, leaving Sir Oliver Hedgestone alone at his desk. His watch beeped. He looked down at the large gold and silver piece. It was a Tarrant, one of the most expensive watch brands in the world. Each one had a pure ruby in the center, and the rarest model—The Aztec Tarrant—also included a piece of Aztec gold. That particular watch had been missing for years, and Sir Oliver Hedgestone had been taking expeditions with a massive exploration team looking for it. He went to Africa, Europe, Russia, China, South America, and even New Jersey, all with no luck. He would find it someday—of that he was certain—even if it was the last thing he ever did.

Hedgestone looked out over his office and admired his other trophies. They were obtained, for the most part, by paying people to take the artifacts from those who found them. He was constantly on the lookout for the newest and latest discoveries someone else had made. Whether it was Roman, Egyptian, Romanian, or from Transylvania, he wanted it. He desired absolutely anything and everything he could get, whether it was weapons, vases, pots, tools, skulls, tablets, or otherwise.

He leaned back in his chair and tapped his desk. A small drawer opened, and inside was a large remote control. He hit a button, and the large bookcase against the wall in front of him started to slide, revealing a 200-inch flat screen television. It had several feeds, all of them playing the news from different parts of the world. He watched for a moment before focusing on the local report. He hit another button, and soon the entire screen consisted of only Lucas Fruber, the local news anchor.

"It seems there will be chaos tonight over Bayside Beach as Ralley's Comet will come completely into our atmosphere and within several miles of the city. There doesn't seem to be any real danger as the comet is not large. Once it enters the atmosphere, it will break up into small pieces that will fall into the ocean. If you're out by the beach at 11:15 p.m. tonight, you should have a great show! Now back to Bob Cotter for the sports."

"This should be a sight," Hedgestone mumbled to himself.

Looking around the room, he noticed a spot on the bookshelf was empty and just big enough for a small piece of comet. He pulled out his cell phone and dialed.

"Sir?" a voice answered.

"Get me the comet."

"Yes, sir."

CHAPTER 6

The dinner table was laden with chicken, potatoes, bread, broccoli, and steamed carrots. Mrs. Calusa poured the water as Mr. Calusa placed the basket of rolls on the table. He leaned over and kissed her on her cheek, and she smiled and kissed him back. As they parted, an older man, who was slightly overweight and balding, appeared in the doorway. He was wearing a black shirt that read "TEAM ADVENTURE CLUB" on the front, and he still had his biker goggles on his forehead.

"Do you have to kiss my sister all the time?" Uncle Max laughed.

"Trust me: it's not all the time," Mr. Calusa said.

"Man, what a night it's going to be! First, a club meeting and then a comet at the beach. It's all so exciting." Uncle Max was loud, and his voice carried. He was constantly excited about everything, and he loved Carrie, Leanne, and Robbie like they were his own children. Robbie walked in, and Uncle Max went nuts. "Robbie! The Robster!" He made his hands into claws and clacked them in Robbie's direction.

Robbie reached out and high fived him, then they did a fist pound and some sort of hand slap routine that was long and complicated. When Leanne walked in, Uncle Max went nuts again. Leanne jumped up and down and dove, hugging Uncle Max as hard as she could.

Carrie slowly walked down the stairs to join the group, wearing dark sunglasses. Uncle Max looked at her and smiled. "Why the shades, rock star?"

"It's a long story."

Uncle Max dipped down, giving her a hug. "You can tell me over dinner."

They all started to dig in, with Carrie explaining what had happened between bites. Robbie filled in the technical bits about what he thought had malfunctioned and how he might be able to fix the glasses.

"I'm really impressed, Robbie. To be able to put those images on the inside of the glasses is fascinating to say the least. It's almost like a HUD," Uncle Max said.

"What's a HUD?" Mrs. Calusa asked.

"That's a heads-up display," Leanne replied. "It's so you don't have to look down at the controls—they are projected directly on the glass. Fighter pilots have them on the inside of their helmets now."

"Robbie, you and I can work together and make our own version of TAC HUD sunglasses." Uncle Max started getting excited.

"No!" Carrie shouted. "My head still hurts a lot. I can still see the faint outline of everything."

Mr. Calusa took a bite of food, chewing slowly before joining the conversation. "So, you made a pair of eyeglasses that calculated the length of an object?"

"Well, yeah. Kind of," Robbie said.

"You kids are fueled by Uncle Max's imagination." Mrs. Calusa shook her head.

"Mom, it's a fact." Carrie pointed to her sunglasses.

"Oh, just like that time you guys found that secret portal to the Bermuda Triangle."

"Yes!" all four of them shouted.

Mr. Calusa almost choked on his milk. He frowned at his wife; perhaps she should stop.

Mrs. Calusa didn't take the hint. "Honestly Maximilian, I don't know why you insist on playing these games."

"Sis, I have explained this to you a *Maximilian* times. We are Team Adventure Club. We seek adventure, fun, excitement, and most of all, treasure, aliens, monsters, and ghosts! I can't do that as a security guard, at least not all the time." He sipped the foam off of his root beer.

"Will you ever grow up?" she asked.

"I hope not, sis. Where's the fun in that?" Uncle Max's watch beeped. "7:30 TAC. Let's get these dishes cleaned up, so we can get to that clubhouse."

With that, everyone but Mr. and Mrs. Calusa sprang from the table. They had a system worked out. Uncle Max would wash while Robbie cleared the table, Carrie would put the leftover food away, and Leanne dried the dishes. They worked fast. Their best record was ten minutes.

It was the only thing Mrs. Calusa loved about the Wednesday night club meeting.

Once the kitchen was spotless, the gang made their way out to the clubhouse. Mrs. Calusa gave them their usual cookie as they headed out. Uncle Max paused in the doorway. "Sandra, why don't you just let the kids have their fun? They're not going to get hurt or anything."

"Max, I know how you were when we were growing up. You made up ridiculous stories about ridiculous things. I just don't want her chasing far-fetched dreams."

"But sis, that's what this world was built on: dreams and far-fetched ideas."

Mrs. Calusa just smiled and shoved her brother out the door.

Carrie, Leanne, and Robbie were already in the clubhouse, which sat between two large oak trees. It was huge and even had electricity. Or, rather, a long extension cord that snaked across the back yard from the garage. Mr. Calusa had ruined four so far because he kept forgetting about them when he mowed the lawn.

Inside, there were several beanbag chairs, two office chairs, a dry-erase board, and an old television with an outdated VCR/DVD combo connected to it—which seemed out of place for all the high-tech gear they had. There was also a small digital video camera on a tripod so they could watch the surveillance footage from their most recent case. Uncle Max was in charge of hooking it all up.

Robbie reached over to the outdated VCR/DVD console, pushing on the top. It opened up and revealed a cubby full of snacks. He took a hand full of chips, shoving them into his mouth. Leanne reached in an pulled out a piece of red licorice, taking a huge bite.

Carrie called the meeting to order, took attendance, and made sure they were all paying attention. "First order of business: Mrs. Keller's three-year-old beagle Pogo has been missing for almost two weeks. I'm a little upset at us for having not found Pogo yet."

"I checked all the kennels in town, and both pounds. Pogo is not there," Robbie reported.

"I put Pogo up on the missing dog Facebook page, but no hits yet," Leanne added to the report.

"Did Mrs. Keller have any enemies?" Uncle Max asked.

"Good question. According to her neighbors, her grandson, Richard, had visited recently and was upset that he couldn't keep the dog." Carrie pointed to the dry-erase board where some notes were listed.

"Where does Richard live?" Leanne asked.

"In Chucca Valley, sixty miles from here." Carrie used her laser pointer to highlight the city on the large map hanging on the wall.

"We can't go there to check it out until the weekend," Robbie said, dejected.

"I can go during the week," Uncle Max chimed in.

"That might work, Uncle Max. Check out the house. He lives with his parents, Jacky and William Harrison. Oh, and he's nine. So be careful; they're squirrely at that age." Suddenly,

Carrie squeezed her eyes shut, then put her head down in her hands. She moaned.

"Indeed, they are. I'll stay at a distance and only survey." Uncle Max looked at his niece, concerned. "Are you okay, Carrie?"

"I still have a wicked headache, and I kind of still see lines, graphs, and numbers." She moaned again, then shook herself. "Okay. Moving on to the second order of business. There will be a comet tonight at 11:15 just over Bay Side Beach. Who's in?"

"Oh, I'd love to, but I have an economics test on Friday. It's ten percent of my grade this quarter. I have to study." Leanne pouted. "Maybe you shouldn't go either with that headache."

"I'm not missing this thing even if my eyes fall out."

The two glared at each other for a moment, but it passed quickly when Robbie jumped in. "I'll go. I'll zipline out to the roof of the shed and meet you in the back alley at 10:25."

"Why so early?" Carrie asked.

"We can't take the scooters. I'm not asking if I can go to the beach at that time of night. My parents will bug-out," Robbie said.

"Good point." Carrie nodded.

"I'm all in. I have to verify this isn't a micro-burst-freezing missile sent here from the planet Ort Ort." Uncle Max's TAC COM beeped. "I could talk to your parents for you if you want." All three just looked at him. "Or maybe not."

He quickly looked at his TAC COM. On the screen was something strange—it seemed to be yelling at him. He looked up at everyone and quickly put his hand behind his back.

"Should you take that, Uncle Max?" Carrie asked.

"What? This? No. Not important. They'll call back," he said in a rush.

The device stopped beeping, and Uncle Max gave a sigh of relief. With the formal part over, the rest of the club members also relaxed.

Carrie went to the dry-erase board and wrote the week's instructions for finding Mrs. Keller's dog while Robbie pulled out the equation glasses and handed them to Uncle Max.

"I can't figure out why they went all crazy."

Uncle Max looked at them for a moment, turning them this way and that. He opened up the arms and tried looking through them without putting them on. He could see that they were still working. Tiny graphs, lines, and numbers were bouncing all over the place, measuring everything. Uncle Max took a deep breath. "Well, here goes nothing." He slipped them on. Everything turned purple for a moment, then he was inundated with information, and no matter what he looked at, it was measured and drawn out. He could only think of one thing to say. "Wow!"

The glasses didn't faze him like they did Carrie. He had seen this kind of craftsmanship before, a long time ago, in a galaxy not so far away. He knew exactly how to control the amount of information he was seeing and when to expect things and when not to. You actually had to look past the lenses if you didn't want to see the information. "Robbie, these are fantastic!"

"Thanks!"

"Why didn't you get sick?" Carrie asked

"I've seen things like this before. These are great! Some of the best I've seen, really. This is exactly the kind of stuff we need for Team Adventure Club! I think I can create a way to have a menu and storage on it, so you can call up just the information you need when you need it. They'll become a large asset to us once they're done. Great job, Robbie!"

CHAPTER 7

It was cold outside. The steam was pouring off of Sir Oliver Hedgestone's bald head in waves. Jenny, in her suit, shivered. She held a briefcase in one hand and a coffee in the other. n the large airplane hangar behind her sat three Learjet's. All three said Hedgestone Enterprises in big letters on the sides. A large Hummer Limousine idled, the motor running.

They watched a smaller aircraft taxi in. Sir Oliver Hedgestone took his coffee and the small warmth it provided—from Jenny.

"Doesn't the night air make you feel vibrant?" He didn't expect an answer, and she was smart enough not to give one. "It just gets into your lungs." He spent several long moments breathing in the cool air before taking a sip and handing the coffee cup back.

Sir Oliver Hedgestone watched as the plane grew nearer. He motioned to two large men in black suits standing in the distance to come closer. These were his bodyguards. Louis, his head bodyguard, was ex-military, ex-CIA, ex-FBI, and ex-personality. As far as anyone could tell, he had never laughed a day in his life. The other man, Mark, was shorter and spoke with a Texan drawl. He was second-in-command, and he was also ex-everything that you could think of.

As they waited, the plane came to a stop, and the door opened. A thin man with a ponytail and a smile as wide as Florida stepped out, coming down the stairs. He was wearing cargo shorts, an open Hawaiian shirt with a t-shirt underneath, a large necklace with a shark's tooth, and sandals. Following him was a shorter, heavier man wearing cargo shorts. The two adventurers—Sam and William—didn't technically work for Sir Oliver Hedgestone, but they did go out and find priceless artifacts for him on a regular basis.

William adjusted his ponytail as he approached. "Mr. Hedgestone!" he exclaimed.

"It's *Sir* Hedgestone," Louis corrected, his voice flat and emotionless.

William looked back at his partner, and they both shrugged. "Okay. Sir Mr. Hedgestone."

"No. Just Sir. It's a title given by the Queen of England," Jenny clarified.

Sam and William both shrugged again. "Sir Hedgestone it is!" Sam said, holding out a metal briefcase.

Sir Oliver Hedgestone nodded to Louis, who stepped closer and motioned to Sam to open the case. Sir Oliver Hedgestone smiled as the contents inside gleamed.

"Now, this was a little trickier to get than we had first thought. It was something of a customs issue as well, Mr. Sir Mr. Hedgestone." William laughed at his own joke.

"Gentlemen, we agreed on a price, regardless of what it cost you to acquire said product. I am only going to pay what we agreed upon," Jenny replied for her employer.

Sir Oliver Hedgestone reached into the case and picked up the large ruby. It was almost the size of his hand. He held it between his thumb and forefinger and admired it for a long moment before returning it to the case. "Leave the money. Let's go," he said, before turning on his heel and walking toward the waiting limousine. The driver quickly opened the door for him as he approached.

Jenny motioned to the men to leave the case. William took the case from Sam and put it on the ground, and only then did Jenny slide a second case toward them. She picked up the one with the ruby and followed her boss. She didn't pay much attention as the adventurers chattered excitedly, counting the wads of cash inside their suitcase.

Getting into the limo, she put Sir Oliver Hedgestone's coffee into a drink warmer and watched as Louis and Mark got into a black sedan waiting next to the limo. Jenny put the case next to her on the seat then pulled out her leather-bound legal pad. She began reviewing the items on her list for the day when her watch beeped. "Sir, it's a quarter to eleven. Did you want to try and make it to Bayside Beach this evening?"

"The night is going splendidly. Yes, let's head to the beach and watch a comet fall. If all goes well, it will land in the sand, and we will be able to collect that as well."

Jenny nodded. "As you wish, sir." She tapped on the privacy window and gave the new instructions to the driver.

CHAPTER 8

Robbie's TAC COM beeped, and he sprang from bed like a ninja. He was already dressed, and he even had his shoes on. He slung his bag onto his back and moved quickly, snapping his zipline handle into place. The cable ran from his window to a large tree in his yard. His parents let him have it because they couldn't disagree that it was handy in case of a fire or other emergencies.

Meanwhile, Carrie was up and playing another round of Pony vs Pony, a popular online game. She had to keep her computer speakers on low so her parents couldn't hear the game and its catchy tune. Then her TAC COM beeped. She made her last move in the game and closed it out. She would have to come back later and beat the pants off of Speedy Lady Lord another time.

Robbie landed with ease on the soft ground and opened the side door to the garage. He looked at his scooter and knew its absence would be a dead giveaway, so he opted for his skateboard. He ran out of the garage and was met by Carrie, who was on her bicycle. She was dressed all in black.

Robbie grinned at her. "You look awesome!"

Carrie smiled. "Thanks!"

"Are you still having headaches?"

"No, they've just stopped, thank god." She tossed him a tow line. "Let's go!"

"No Leanne, huh?" Robbie asked as he made sure he had a good grip on the rope.

"Nope. That's okay though. This isn't officially a Team Adventure Club assignment."

Robbie held on tightly as they set off. His skateboard was slightly different than most; he had two aluminum canisters, with leather straps holding them in place on the rear and a metal pedal on the front that looked like a bare foot, although he wasn't using them at the moment. There was also a hose that went from each of the canisters to another metal canister on the side which connected to the pedal electronically. The canister read: TURBO BOOST.

Carrie's bicycle was also modified. She had a gas engine she could switch on that could get the bike up to twenty miles an hour. But tonight, she was pedaling. It was quieter, and it was an easy route—the whole way to the beach was downhill.

Leanne sat at her desk looking over her economics book. She hated every minute of it. She kept falling asleep, her head jerking each time she snapped awake. She wiped a thin line of drool off her chin and rubbed her face. Maybe she needed a break. She tapped her keyboard to check the tracker following the comet.

She wanted to go to the beach, but if she failed the test on Friday, she could only get a "C" in the class. She just couldn't miss this though. Decision made, she slipped out of the house and hopped on her scooter, speeding her way down the sidewalk in no time flat.

Uncle Max was already at the beach. He had a telescope set up and linked to his industrial-strength laptop in its rubber-encased case. All his monitoring equipment was carefully laid out on a table: a satellite communications switchboard plugged into a miniature satellite array; a printer spitting out readings and signal messages from the National Radio Astronomy Observatory Station in New Mexico; a flat screen monitor with a grid tracking the comet and another giving weather reports; and a short-wave radio tuned into a local news station. He was more than set. He used his binoculars to scan the night sky, but there was still no sign of the so-called comet. He changed the settings on the binoculars to read for thermal imaging. Still nothing.

He sat back down in his beach chair, popped open a root beer, and unwrapped an oatmeal cream pie. He noticed that people were starting to make their way onto the beach. Checking his TAC COM, he saw that the team was almost there. All three of them.

Uncle Max started to become antsy as people approached his table, asking questions. He quickly covered his equipment with a tarp and crawled under it so that no one could see him either. His TAC COM beeped.

"Uncle Max, where are you?" Robbie's face popped up on the small screen.

"I'm under a tarp. I'm starting to feel compromised!"

"What are you talking about?" Robbie asked.

"There's too many people here now."

"How many?" Robbie was having trouble watching the monitor and watching where he was going on his scooter.

Uncle Max peeked his head out from under the tarp and looked around quickly. "Four or five now."

"Okay, hold tight. We're about two minutes away."

"I know. I have you on monitor," Uncle Max said. "Over and out!" Robbie's face froze on Uncle Max's screen in a weird, contorted way, giving Robbie a large nose and huge teeth. Uncle Max screenshot the image, laughing.

At the same time, Leanne was breezing down the boardwalk. She made it to the beach and found Uncle Max's combat SUV and his makeshift tent, but she didn't see Carrie or Robbie's scooters. She made her way down the ramp to the beach until the scooter started having trouble in the deep sand. She parked it at the nearest bike rack and locked it down.

Before she had a chance to start for the tent, Carrie popped out from behind the SUV. "About time!"

Leanne jumped in surprise and hugged her friend. Then she noticed Robbie standing with Max, who, even from a distance, looked nervous. They walked arm-in-arm to where the boys were waiting, and Leanne got a full view of Uncle Max's setup. Robbie had convinced him to put aluminum poles up, so that the tarp acted like an awning over the table full of consoles and satellites.

Uncle Max sat in his chair with a strange device on his head. Attached to it were a pair of goggles. His right hand rested on a joystick that moved a telescope he had set up several feet away. He flipped up the visor, smiled at Leanne, then flipped it back down. "I'm trying to focus the Z-1 Telescope on the comet, but I can't seem to find it. It has to be within the Earth's atmosphere by now. I mean, it's almost 11:15. Where is it?"

Carrie and Leanne simultaneously lifted their official TAC-oculars and scanned the sky. These were regular binoculars with a sticker on the side that read Team Adventure Club. Both noted that they only saw clouds and stars. Robbie inputted the numbers from one of the printers into a laptop Uncle Max had set up, careful to record the data properly.

Carrie lowered her TAC-oculars just in time to see a limousine pull up. She wondered who it was. A black car pulled in behind the limo. Two large men got out and walked to the limo, opening the door for a short, bald man in a suit and a very pretty woman. Several people gawked at him, and one man even walked up to shake his hand. He was promptly ushered away by one of the two men from the car.

Carrie snapped a picture with her camera then pulled the memory card out and put it into her TAC COM. She enlarged the picture of the man and then double-tapped to start a search. As soon as the internet activated, it recognized the image.

A news article popped up. It went on and on about Sir Oliver Hedgestone and all the different types of companies he owned, from oil rigs to military weapons to service organizations. He was worth billions. Carrie continued to scroll, and more information popped up about his wife's mysterious disappearance.

"What did you find?" Leanne asked, causing Uncle Max and Robbie to look up.

"Oh, nothing. Just a rich billionaire with his limo on the beach." Carrie flipped her TAC COM so Leanne could see it.

Uncle Max moved closer to skim the article, then looked up the beach at the limo. "He's a tyrant!"

"Because he has money?" Carrie asked.

"No because he just fired like two hundred people from one of his companies last week," Uncle Max said. "He said he was putting more robots in his warehouses."

"Robots are cool!" Robbie said from his spot beneath the tarp.

"Be that as it may, it's not nice to replace hard working people with electronics. Trust me." Uncle Max grunted, lifting his binoculars. He scanned the limo and the people around it. "Hedgestone has his fingers in the government too—making personal shuttle carriers for military personnel. They want to start the first Space Army. It's not going to work! They have no idea what they're in for."

Carrie and Leanne looked at each other and smirked. Carrie loved her uncle, and no matter what, she wanted to believe his stories like being abducted and saving Earth from an interstellar war, but sometimes she even doubted him herself. He did, however, know a lot about new technology, and he built most of the stuff they used in the club. He knew a lot about space travel too, more than even her science teacher. But like her mom always said: "You just don't know how much he's making up!" Could Uncle Max just be a crazy goofball? Possibly. But either way, Carrie loved him. He was *her* goofball.

Uncle Max was busy studying Hedgestone when the monitors started to beep and buzz.

"There's something coming!" Robbie cried enthusiastically.

CHAPTER 9

Burning through the atmosphere, the small comet sped toward Bellevue Heights. It was a hard rock with large craters all over it that glowed a dazzling, bright white. Dark smoke billowed off the back as debris ripped off the rock and evaporated into moisture. The tip was superheated, but instead of burning red, it burned blue.

As it broke through the clouds, something strange happened.

The comet started spinning and a metal extension popped out. A bright blue light shone from inside, and on each side, a wing-shaped panel opened. The comet started to slow down as the wings tilted slightly.

Uncle Max watched on the monitors as he zoomed in on his Z-1 telescope. As he noticed the wings, his mouth fell open. He looked up over his telescope, and he could barely see it with his naked eye. Carrie and Leanne, on the other hand, zoomed in on their TAC-oculars but could just see a blue ball hurling through the air with a large streaming dark tail.

Uncle Max darted to the back of his SUV and pulled out a large green trunk, dragging it back through the sand. He knelt down and stared at the digital combination lock, his mind suddenly going blank. He couldn't remember the combination. Carrie and Leanne were too busy to notice he wasn't doing anything.

Robbie was in awe as he watched the comet up close on the monitor. When he zoomed in, he saw a small flag on the comet that read: GREETINGS FROM THE PLANET ORT ORT. This gave him pause.

Most of the beachgoers could barely make out the comet but were starting to point at the sky and murmur to each other. Sir Oliver Hedgestone stood with his hands behind his back as he watched. He was wearing dark sunglasses, but unlike the other watchers, he could see the comet perfectly. Numbers scrolled on both lenses, calculating mass, velocity, and other statistics. He could also see the message on the flag. "Get Commander Collins on the phone. Now. We have an interesting specimen incoming, and an offer on the table," he said.

Yes sir!" Jenny quickly pulled out her phone.

Miles away from the beach, the military office was crowded with personnel looking at giant monitors and sitting behind desks with headsets on. There were fifty people, all either on the phone or talking into their headsets. The double doors to the room swung open, and a small man in military dress walked in with a large red satellite phone. "Commander Collins, sir?"

A hulking Commander turned around. He was six feet tall, with a flat top haircut, huge chin, and long sideburns that connected to his even fuller mustache. "You walk into my office in the middle of a training exercise, you'd better be here to tell me we're under attack by aliens or giant robots!" he snarled.

The messenger held his eyes closed and handed him the phone. "It's... Sir Oliver Hedgestone, sir."

Commander Collins snatched the phone. "DISMISSED!" He lifted the phone, watching the soldier scurry off. "What do you have for me?"

"Hold please." He recognized the voice as Hedgestone's current personal assistant. The Commander was often called by Hedgestone when he needed some help only the military could provide. He was often called on for more ... delicate operations, and he was paid large sums of money to do it. In return, Hedgestone only called when it was important. This time was no different.

"We have something alien, Commander."

"How alien?" He raised an eyebrow at the thought.

"From another planet alien. I would hate to think it's an attack on the human race."

"Where?"

"Right in my backyard, serendipitously enough, riding on the back of a comet. I've already put my team on it. We will try and collect it for observation." Sir Oliver Hedgestone's voice was smooth and controlled.

"We'll leave in ten."

"Excellent." Commander Collins chewed on his cheek for a moment, contemplating his next move.

Collins looked around at the personnel in his office. "Jones, Tarrant, Khars, Bohn, Buchanan, and Summers. We head out in five in full recon gear! Let's move people!" he bellowed. "We've got an intergalactic threat on our hands!"

A few hundred yards down the beach from the limousine, Uncle Max stared at the lock, trying to remember the combination. He tried to remember what he had been doing when he was locking everything inside of this certain case. *Was I in Africa? No. China? No. Bermuda? Yes, Bermuda, right after TAC fought that giant squid.*

As Carrie and Leanne watched, two silent helicopters appeared in the sky. They were huge and had Hedgestone Enterprises on the side in dark letters. The side door opened, and two men in dark gear clipped their ropes to a guide and hung outside, using the ropes as safety harnesses. The pilot maneuvered into position, obviously trying to line up with the incoming comet. The second helicopter did the same. As the helicopters got closer, one of the men hanging out of the door brandished a long device with a clamp on one end, while another held a canister with a biohazard symbol on it.

"Do you see this?" Carrie couldn't believe her eyes.

"Hedgestone Enterprises?" Leanne read, her eyes glued to the scene as well.

"He's here for the comet. They're going to try and catch it!" Carrie shouted.

Uncle Max, still crouching before the locked case, abruptly stood up. "What? No. They can't. No one can touch it!"

He looked at the closed case, then across the beach to where Hedgestone was standing. He didn't have time to warn them. He had to make a choice. He knelt down again and punched in the code.

As the first helicopter approached the comet, the team let their lead lines go and dropped in the air. They steadied themselves over the comet, the pilot matching their speed. They were only a few feet from the glowing alien rock. As they got a closer look, one of them noticed the wings, but by that time, it was too late.

"We might have an issue," he radioed to the others.

"What kind of issue?" the pilot responded.

"Not sure. Team two, be ready."

"Team two, ready," came the reply.

The soldier reached for the comet and managed to get the rope around it without touching it. He slowly closed the device around the comet and breathed easier. "Package secure."

Suddenly, the clamp started to freeze. The ice worked its way up the metal pole to his hand. Before he could do anything, his arm was frozen and, in a blink, he was a solid block of ice. He didn't even have a chance to radio in for help.

"We have a problem!" his teammate screamed into the radio as the ice came for him, too. He watched in horror as it spread up his limbs and consumed him. The ice coated the helicopter itself; the blades stopped mid-spin and it plummeted to the ground.

Carrie and Leanne watched as the helicopter glowed an icy blue and then started to fall out of the sky. The comet burst through the device around it and continued on its course. The second helicopter pulled away, not even making an attempt to catch the comet themselves.

It was headed right for the bay. Carrie and Leanne followed it with their TAC-oculars, watching in slack-jawed amazement as it hit the water, freezing it instantly. The comet bounced off the ice and back into the air before coming down again to hit a boat. That was also frozen solid, followed by the boardwalk. People ran, but everyone who got too close was frozen as well. As it continued to bounce, it headed right for Sir Oliver Hedgestone.

He jumped back into the limo with Jenny right behind him, and they sped off down the beach. In their haste, they hit another car parked in the sand but kept going. People jumped out of their way. The limo hit another vehicle and spun, giving Jenny a good view of the chaos out the window. She watched a nice young couple freeze solid. "It's freezing everything!"

"It seems it is," Sir Oliver Hedgestone said emotionless

The limo driver tried best not to hit things, but the ice was starting to catch up to them.

The limo driver tried his best not to hit things; it slowed them down and the ice was getting closer in the rearview mirror. He turned hard up a ramp, trying to get off the beach, but the wheels had already started to freeze.

Sir Oliver Hedgestone grabbed Jenny, and they jumped out. They ran right toward Carrie and the rest of Team Adventure Club. Carrie watched the billionaire run toward her, her TAC-oculars dangling from the lanyard around her neck. Jenny, lagging behind, froze. Sir Oliver Hedgestone leapt into midair, but he, too, started to freeze. The briefcase he was holding flipped open and a huge red ruby flew through the air.

Carrie watched as the ruby spun through the air. Then she realized the ice was coming right for her and the rest of Team Adventure Club. She grabbed Leanne and they held each other, afraid they were going to freeze.

Uncle Max slammed a canister into the sand. "Cover your eyes!" That was the only warning they got before the world exploded around them.

Carrie slowly opened her eyes to see a glowing force field around them. The ice moved up and around the force field but left them safe. It was only as the ruby bounced off with a *tink* that she realized the ruby itself was also unaffected by the ice. It bounced off the ice-coated sand and spun out onto the frozen ocean.

CHAPTER 10

The sunny city of Bellevue Heights was frozen solid in a matter of minutes. There wasn't a person, animal, or building that wasn't encased in a block of ice. If Carrie and the gang didn't figure this out fast, the entire world could be frozen forever.

Most of the people were completely unaware of what had happened. Across town, Debra Valentine was sleeping comfortably in her bed, pink sleep mask pulled over her eyes, when she was encased in a cocoon of solid ice.

Inside their bubble, the smoke settled, but Carrie still held tightly to Leanne. Robbie stood with one foot up and his eyes covered. Uncle Max breathed heavily. Finally, Carrie and Leanne slowly let go of each other and stood up. "What was that?" Carrie asked.

"It's called an Omni-Directional Anti-Debris Deflector, otherwise known as the OD-ADD." Uncle Max looked around at the bubble, pleased with himself.

"Not *that*. The thing bouncing around freezing our town!" Carrie looked out at the frozen landscape

"That was bad news. I believe it is a missile from the planet Ort Ort. I think they may have just declared war on Earth."

Robbie, Carrie, and Leanne looked at him with their mouths open. The only upside was that they finally knew, definitively, that all of his stories about fighting aliens were true. Robbie found his voice first. "What?" he croaked.

"Robbie, my boy, you have no idea what awaits us off this planet—things so unimaginable and amazing you would need six lifetimes to look at it all." Uncle Max s sorted through his tools.

"So, when you said you fought to save Earth when you were a teenager? That was all true?" Carrie tried to focus on her breathing.

"I wouldn't lie about such things. I was a hero once. Out there, I'm the Captain of a starship! Here, I'm a man-child that people make fun of. We're so archaic here compared to other civilizations on other planets. But humans are not ready for that kind of knowledge, other species of life living on other planets for millions of years. It changes your outlook on the universe. It changes everything."

"I'm sorry," Carrie said, tears starting to well up. *How did I ever doubt him?*

"Why? It's not your fault. Humans will never have any idea just how close they came to extinction. It was me—a fifteen-year-old—who fought the intergalactic battle for Earth and stopped it. All I was left with was my word. But I know what I did: how I managed to lead a squadron of fighters against evil aliens and won. It's always been enough for me."

Uncle Max lifted his shirt to show them a huge scar that ran from his shoulder to his elbow. "I got this when I went toe to toe with B'gan Kon Re Thras, the leader of the Salutatorians, a very evil race of aliens from 1,000 light years away."

"Mom said you got that falling off the roof," Carrie said.

"I almost died. The Guthernians, this very friendly race of aliens from Rog'ath, a planet like fifty light years away, saved my life. See, they were the good guys. Without me, we all would have died. Without them, I would have died. When I returned, we couldn't let anyone know what happened I have been sworn to secrecy by my bond. So as a sign of respect, I was gifted knowledge far more advanced than the smartest human on earth. With that knowledge, I still protect earth. And I pass the knowledge on to you. By making killer equipment. Anyway, They had a huge celebration for me when I left. I was a grand hero. I hid the scar for a while, and when someone finally asked, I said I got it years ago falling off the roof. No one said otherwise."

"So how do we stop this ice missile?" Carrie asked, standing up straighter. She was going to follow in Uncle Max's footsteps and be a great hero of Earth, too.

"That is a good question." Uncle Max pulled out a long, thin device from his weapons belt, turning the end of it. He pushed a red button and it hummed to life. Flipping the dark part of his goggles down, he pointed the device at the shield. "Cover your eyes, kids."

The device popped to life and started cutting through both the shield and the ice, etching out a nice doorway for them to walk through. The thick chunk of ice slammed onto the frozen beach with a loud thud. As they stepped out into the world again, the temperature changed drastically; it was cold. Carrie rubbed her arms as her breath escaped in a cloud of steam. Leanne and Robbie shivered, hopping around and rubbing their arms to get warm again.

"Over here, guys." Uncle Max gestured for them to follow him to his van. With the laser, he etched the doors free and pulled a large trunk out from behind the backseat. Opening it he pulled out winter gear—all labeled with the TAC logo—and passed them around.

Once he was dressed in appropriate clothes, Robbie looked around. "Ah man! My skateboard is frozen!"

"Everything is frozen, Robbie!" Carrie yelled.

"Not everything." He pointed to the ruby, sitting on the frozen ocean.

Carrie turned to look, then remembered seeing it fly out of the case Sir Oliver Hedgestone had been carrying. She carefully made her way out over the ice to retrieve it.

"Look how big it is, Uncle Max!" She held it up with both hands.

Uncle Max put on his own jacket as he made his way over to her. "Interesting." He accepted it from Carrie and examined it closely. It was large for a ruby—or any other gem for that matter. The fact that it was still fine when everything else—everything he had fought to save so many years ago—was encased in ice meant something. He handed it to Robbie for safekeeping. "Put this in your bag and keep it close. Let's go see the damage."

Robbie pulled out a small multitool and flipped it open to reveal a hammer. He slammed it into the ice covering Leanne's scooter, but it just bounced off the slick surface and hit him square in the forehead. Robbie's feet went straight up into the air, and he landed on his back. He moaned.

"Well, looks like we're walking." Uncle Max shrugged. "Robbie, get up. This isn't the time to be taking naps."

Carrie had moved to look at the frozen billionaire and couldn't put her finger on why she felt like there was something strange about him. Perhaps she had seen him before? *But where?*

Uncle Max came over, putting an arm around her. "What's wrong?"

"I feel like I know him."

Sir Oliver Hedgestone stared back at them from inside his frozen prison. He couldn't make out their faces very well since the ice distorted his vision, but he made a note of everything he could. If only he could get out of the ice, he would get his ruby back.

"I've just got a bad feeling about this guy," Carrie murmured as they all started the trek back toward town.

CHAPTER 11

The members of the Team Adventure Club looked around in awe as they wandered around town. Everything and everyone was frozen solid. It seemed to be getting colder by the minute too.

They hopped a fence and started on a trek through the backyards of the local neighborhoods. They hopped fence after fence, and even walked across someone's frozen pool. When they finally reached the house, they found it, too, covered in a layer of ice. Uncle Max pulled out the small laser gun and started cutting around the door. The entire door—along with a two-inch-thick ice block—fell back into the house with a thud.

Carrie shook her head at her uncle, knowing her mother was going to be furious with a hole in the wall, but she peered inside. The house seemed quiet, and her parents were clearly not in the foyer. She quickly went looking for her parents, finding her father looking in the bathroom mirror and brushing his teeth. Her mother was downstairs wearing bunny slippers and a bathrobe, a basket of laundry balanced on her hip. Carrie spoke to her a few times, only getting a deep echoing thud in return.

Then Carrie noticed that her mother's eyes were moving. "Mom? Can you hear me?"

Her mother shot her a look. Carrie shouted to Max, bringing him rushing over. "I think she can hear me!" They stared at each other and the mother-shaped ice block for a moment. "Should we cut her out?"

Max looked at his sister for a long moment. "Best not," he sighed.

Carrie swallowed but nodded. "Yeah, she's safer in the ice." She turned to the ice block, putting one hand over her mother's frozen hand. "Mom, we will get you out of this. It's an alien attack. Don't worry. We will be right back!"

She ran upstairs and let out a grunt of frustration at finding all her clothes frozen too. She yelled again for Uncle Max, who made his way up the stairs, avoiding the slippery patches. He used his laser gun to shoot the closet a few times, freeing her clothes rack. Incidentally, a few of her shirts caught on fire. She yelped and rushed to put it out. That done, she was finally able to liberate her two biggest, fluffiest winter coats. She held them both up to show Leanne, who had come up to see what the commotion was all about. "Red or blue?"

"Red!" Leanne grinned as Carrie tossed her the coat.

Back outside and much warmer, they made their way up the street. Suddenly, four large black helicopters flew overhead. "Holy cow! Who are they?" Carrie whispered as they ducked behind a frozen car.

"I was afraid of this. The military is already here. Which means we've got about an hour to find the alien weapon and destroy it before they get their hands on it." Uncle Max watched the helicopters disappear over the hill.

"Why do we need to destroy it?" Leanne asked as they continued on their way.

"If the military gets their hands on it, they will try to use it against our enemies."

"So?" Robbie looked at him, genuinely confused.

"If the weapon gets into our enemies' hands instead, the whole planet is doomed. It's better if no one has it," Uncle Max pointed out. "Let's get off the street. We have to move under cover now."

They made it to Robbie's house unnoticed. Max stopped just outside the door, looking off in the direction the helicopters had disappeared to. It was a good guess that the military was setting up a temporary base not too far away; several helicopters hovered over one area, and they could see men rappelling down out of them.

Max pulled out a small plastic contact lens case. He put the lenses in, blinking a few times to settle them and activate the technology. They magnified his vision, allowing him to zoom in and out by blinking. Max watched the military men pulling out equipment as they began setting up their camp. This was going to be a race to try and get to the weapon before anyone else.

"Max, we need the laser!" Robbie called from inside the house, shaking him out of his musings

Blinking a few times to return the lens to regular vision, he headed inside to help the final member of the team get his winter gear unfrozen. He found him looking longingly around the room. "It's all ruined. All my comics. All my posters. All ruined," Robbie groaned.

Max patted him on the shoulder, both observing a moment of silence for the lost precious reading materials.

Finally, Robbie sighed. "C'mon! Let's go do whatever it is we're going to stop this stupid freeze rocket piece of junk." As he quickly walked across the landing, it was obvious he had forgotten that the floor was icy; he slipped and suddenly plunged down the staircase and straight out the front door. Carrie and Leanne could only watch, eyes wide, as Robbie went sliding past them.

Both of them looked up at Max, who was more carefully coming down the stairs. "We need to stop him. He could slide for days!" he exclaimed.

"Days?!" Carrie's eyes widened.

"Well, maybe not *days*. But he very well could slide into the next county."

Meanwhile, Robbie was trying to maintain his composure as he accelerated down the street and through town. He tried using his feet as a brake, but it was no use. He then tried to grab something as he zipped along, but that proved to be unhelpful as well; everything was still covered in ice and just slipped right out of his hands. He decided to focus on where exactly he was going. It took a few heartbeats before he registered what he was seeing. The ice had made a ramp of sorts off of the water tower, and he was headed right for it.

Robbie watched helplessly as he slid toward impending doom. He hit the ice ramp and was shot out over the top of the water tower, screaming and flailing. He tried turning his body so he could see where he might land, but just as he got himself turned around, he started the falling portion of this little trip. He was headed right back toward the slide. He came down faster than he went up and was jettisoned back the way he came.

Down the street, Max, Leanne, and Carrie watched. "We've got to do something," Max said, watching Robbie start his return voyage at twice the speed he had when he left.

They all looked around but saw no immediate solutions. As Robbie came barreling by, they had no choice but to jump out of the way. They could only watch helplessly as he hit the side of a house and was launched upside down toward another house, which launched him back down the street. Robbie hit a trash can and immediately did a ninety-degree ping, shooting across the street to another trash can, ponging off that and headed toward a mailbox.

"I feel like I'm in a pinball machine!" he cried.

This time, as he bounced around, they positioned themselves right in his path. Max dropped to his knees and assumed a catcher's stance, but Carrie pulled him right back up again. "Uncle Max, that won't work; it will just cause one of you to get hurt! We need redirection. If his trajectory and speed can be matched by opposite trajectory and reduced speed, we can slow him down. We have to decrease his inertia exponentially," Carrie said.

Leanne's mouth fell open in shock

"Science guys. C'mon." Carrie shrugged. She looked down the street and, all of a sudden, she could see in "math vision" again including the distance of Robbie from her, the curvature of the streetlights and trees, and even the angle she needed to create triangles from those positions. "Uncle Max, shoot the ice off that tree branch!"

Once he did, she started gesturing quickly. "Do you have any rope or elastic?"

He dug around his pockets, pulling out a ball of rubber bands. "What about this?"

"That won't work. We need a thick rope or net to snag Robbie."

"This has the tensile strength of a dying sun. It can stop a freight train at full speed," he insisted, tossing it to Carrie.

"It's exceptionally light." She gave him a skeptical look.

"Space Wire," Max explained with a smirk.

Carrie shrugged and went to work, quickly making a snare of sorts for Robbie to get caught in. "Okay, we need to make a ramp with a curvature of thirty-two degrees and negative invert of sixteen degrees with a forty-five-degree angle at the top for him to shoot into the air."

"On it!" Max shouted. He started shooting the ice with his laser, creating a pile of slush in the street. He and Leanne pushed it together like playdoh until they had constructed a solid ramp.

As Robbie came speeding onto the street, he hit the Space Wire. It snagged him, his momentum shot him up over the ramp and wrapped him around the tree. He spun over and over until there was no more slack, and he was finally still.

Bound to the tree, Robbie was motionless for a moment, blinking at all of them. "THAT WAS THE MOST AMAZING ROLLER COASTER IN THE WORLD! WAAAA-WHOOOOO!" He did as much of a happy dance as he could while tied down, laughing. "You should have seen how high I went into the air! It was amazing! I could see the next town!"

Max shot the wire, freeing Robbie who slid to the ground. Robbie shook his head. "Guys! You should try that! Holy moly! It was ... the best thing ever!"

Carrie and Leanne shook their heads no at him while Uncle Max helped him to his feet. "Oh, and I saw Mrs. Keller's dog Pogo! Don't let me forget that," he added as they walked away.

CHAPTER 12

A large Hedgestone-owned B-45 Pelican Helicopter landed on the ice several yards away from the impromptu military base. The rear door opened, and ten soldiers got out, followed by Commander Collins. He popped a cigar in his mouth, lighting it as he strolled down the ramp.

In a field not far away, three military jeeps, six military TR-99 SuperCobra attack helicopters, two EW-134 Apache Fire Strikes speed choppers, and various other modes of transportation were lined up, waiting for his arrival.

First Lieutenant Tarrant came to attention and saluted smartly. "Commander, welcome to Rosewood."

"You boys go set up your stations, and I'll see you in a few. Do me proud, men!" Commander Collins bellowed.

"You heard him, men! Khars and Buchanan, move the gear to the armory. Jones, Bohn and Summers, follow me." Tarrant barked out orders, getting everyone moving swiftly to their assigned tasks.

As the grunts scattered, another soldier came closer. "Commander Collins! I'm Captain

Antonio Hernandez, glad to meet you. If you'll follow me, sir, I will escort you to the command tent."

As they walked, Commander Collins took a deep breath. "I miss the smell of wet canvas and weapons."

"Yes, sir. It's a distinct smell."

They arrived at the largest tent in the complex, located in the very center of the camp. Two soldiers flanked the entrance, standing guard.

The captain gave another salute before heading back to his own duties. As he entered, Commander Collins was met by two older men in military uniforms. He saluted them, nodding as they returned the greeting. "Colonel Richardson, Colonel Frierson," he said, by way of greeting. "Good to see you."

Pleasantries over, Colonel Richardson tossed a packet of papers onto the table. Top Secret was stamped on the cover. "This is a mess on a global level, Collins. We have to keep this under wraps. No one must know about this."

Commander Collins opened up the packet, skimming the contents. He paused when he came to a sheet of codes for a nuclear strike, with the words OPERATION CLEAN HOUSE at the top. He raised an eyebrow and tilted the sheet so the colonels could see. "Operation Clean House?"

"You have twelve hours to sort this mess out, find the alien artifact, and get your soldiers out of here. Then Mr. Clean comes in," Colonel Frierson said.

"And the residents of the town?"

"In war—be it domestic, international or galactic—we risk collateral damage. The needs of the many outweigh the needs of the few. A certain number of civilian casualties are expected. We have run the numbers, and the predicted losses are acceptable." Colonel Frierson lit up a pipe, taking a long drag.

Commander Collins took a drag of his own cigar before nodding. "Consider it done," He continued flipping through the paperwork, pulling out one titled Complete Deniability.

Colonel Frierson noted what he was looking at and nodded. "That's insurance. Once we nuke the town, we'll say it was a gas main leak. We will, of course, be very sorry for everyone's loss."

"The press secretary is already working on a speech for the president for tomorrow," Colonel Richardson added.

"War! It's a damn shame it doesn't happen all the time!" Commander Collins bounced on his toes.

"Sergeant, with that attitude, you'll be a colonel before you know it." Colonel Frierson clapped him on the back before following his fellow colonel out of the tent, leaving Commander Collins to his work.

He left the tent as well, and he made his way across the camp to the communication tents. First Lieutenant Tarrant was inside the main pavilion waiting for him. "Sergeant, communications are a go, and connection with the Hedgestone Satellite has been established. However, we have not secured communication with Sir Oliver Hedgestone himself."

"If you can't establish communication with him, then get your men out there and find him."

"We have already triangulated his location, sir." One of the men manning the monitors pointed to a screen. "He seems to be sitting on the beach. He hasn't moved in twenty minutes."

"If you know where he is, then send someone to go get him," Commander Collins snapped.

CHAPTER 13

Team Adventure Club made their way across town, bypassing major roads and cutting through back alleys and side streets as they worked their way to the military camp. They were amazed that one small alien projectile could do so much damage. Every structure, person, vehicle, and thing was covered in a thick sarcophagus of ice.

Robbie's wrist communicator suddenly beeped; the radar showed an oncoming vehicle headed their way. "Everybody down!" They all dove behind ice-laden bushes on the side of the road, waiting until long after the Jeep cruised past to re-emerge.

"That was close!" Leanne stared long after the Jeep's tail lights had disappeared over the horizon. It has gone in the direction of the beach.

Once they were within a few blocks of the camp, they started to hear the commotion of the busy soldiers. The ambient light coming off the base camp gave an eerie glow to this side of town. Max looked at his TAC COM checking for movement nearby. "Coast is clear."

They kept moving, sticking to the shadows to avoid being noticed. Finally, they made it to a huge house just across the street from the base camp, where they took a moment to regroup. "Uncle Max, what's the plan once we get in?" Carrie asked.

"We find the alien device."

"Then what? We can't touch it, remember?" Leanne rubbed at her arms. The temperature was continuing to drop as time went on.

"I haven't figured that part out yet," Uncle Max admitted with a sigh.

"Well, if we can't touch it, then that means the military can't touch it either," Robbie pointed out.

"True." Uncle Max patted him on the back. "I could get next to it and toss an OD-ADD down. Then it would be contained inside."

"With *you* inside?" Carrie asked. "You would be stuck inside your magic shield bubble forever!"

Uncle Max started to respond, then froze. "Shhh." He motioned to everyone to freeze. His TAC COM didn't show anything, but he didn't want to risk it.

"Did you hear footsteps?" Leanne whispered.

It was too late to answer her. Uncle Max turned to find a team of armed men Carrie and Leanne both screamed, and Robbie smacked his communicator. "I thought you said these things detected life forms, Max!"

"Freeze!" one of the soldiers yelled.

They all stopped moving, that is, until Robbie began giggling. "Something funny, boy?" The soldier glared at him.

"You said 'freeze.' *Everything* is frozen. Classic!" Robbie continued to chuckle.

Carrie nudged him, giving him a glare.

"Everyone shut up and stop moving!" the soldier yelled again. He motioned to one of his comrades. "Call this in. We need transport."

"Listen, can't you let the kids go and just take me in?" Uncle Max peered at the name patch sewn onto the soldier's uniform. "Mr. Pegg?"

"It's Military Police Officer Pegg, and I'm afraid not. We have to take you all in. I'll make sure you're treated right." When MP Officer Pegg looked at Carrie and Leanne, his face and voice softened a bit. "Ladies, it's okay. We're not going to hurt you. We're just on a routine surveillance mission. As you can see, something very strange is going on."

They waited for a few minutes until another Jeep arrived. "I'm going to need all of you to get in, please." Officer Pegg gestured to the car.

"It's okay, guys. Let's do this and they'll let us go in a while," Uncle Max said.

Robbie raised his eyebrows, but he didn't comment. This wasn't the first time Team Adventure Club had been taken into custody by a military unit. Several months ago, they were on a mission in Mexico researching the Mayan pyramids and found what Carrie still believed to be the entrance to an underground city leading to the center of earth. Before they could explore, they had been stopped by the Mexican government and politely asked to leave the country.

"Remember when we ran into the Mexican Military?" Robbie said as he stepped into the passenger truck.

Suddenly, Carrie realized where she knew the frozen man from. He was the same guy who had been with the Mexican officials. It had to be! She remembered his bald head and his nose. She kept quiet about her revelation as they all boarded the transport vehicle.

The Jeep headed into the camp, and Max paid close attention to how it was all laid out. He noted a group of spotlights trained on an object: the sphere! Surrounding it, there were close to twenty soldiers frozen in place, each one bent over as if they had tried to pick it up. Then the Jeep turned a corner, and he lost sight of the artifact. He went back to cataloging each tent, truck, and landmark along the way.

They finally arrived at a small tent near the center of camp, where they were directed to disembark. "Stand in line and don't move," MP Officer Pegg said. He mumbled something into his radio, but it was too soft for any of TAC to make out. Finally, MP Officer Pegg nodded and signed off. "Officer Green, please take the young man into tent six."

"Wait. What?" Robbie's eyes went wide.

"Don't worry. It's just protocol."

"Really? To take a twelve-year-old boy into a military tent alone?" Uncle Max moved closer to Robbie, trying to look protective.

"We have to locate his guardian. Unless that's you?"

"Well, technically no," Uncle Max said.

"Are you any of these children's guardian?" MP Officer Green pulled out a notebook.

"He's my uncle," Carrie chimed in. "These are my friends."

MP Officer Pegg nodded, gesturing for Officer Green to escort Robbie to the tent. "It'll be fine, son. Just go with this officer."

Before Robbie could get sarcastic, two female officers approached. MP Officer Pegg gestured to Carrie and Leanne. "MP Officer Cardone and MP Officer Humphrey, take these two young ladies into tent four."

"No. I want to stay with my Uncle Max." Carrie grabbed Max's arm.

"I'm sorry, but for now that isn't possible." MP Officer Pegg gave her another kind look.

"These children were put under my temporary care by their parents. I won't allow them to be taken from me. It would be very irresponsible of me," Uncle Max said firmly. He held out his arms, and all of TAC huddled close.

"I understand, but I'm just doing my job," MP Officer Pegg noted. "Right now, I have orders to send you to three different tents."

"MP Officer Pegg, I respect the military and the police, but if any of these children leave my sight for one second, I will call down a wrath of devastation on your head" Uncle Max held his chin up high.

"What are you saying exactly?" MP Officer Pegg's eyes narrowed, and he suddenly looked less friendly.

"Exactly as it sounded."

"I can put you in federal prison for the rest of your life. You know that, right?"

"You try and do anything to these kids, and prison won't be enough for me. I know some very influential people!" Uncle Max pulled himself up to his full height.

"Take him to tent ten." MP Officer Pegg rolled his eyes and gestured to another officer who had been standing by.

"I'm warning you." Uncle Max knew it was hopeless, but at least it was distraction enough that none of them were searched. The soldiers grabbed them and started dragging them all to separate tents. That was something. For now.

CHAPTER 14

The tent was bright and smelled like old shoes. Robbie sat behind a huge foldaway table, a single plastic glass of water in front of him. He was busy looking around cataloging everything he could when a man wearing a military uniform and huge brown glasses strolled in. His hair was thinning, combed over to hide a shiny bald spot. The officer sat down in front of Robbie, placing a yellow folder on the table between them. He stared for a moment, and Robbie stared right back. Finally, he flipped open the folder and cleared his throat. "Robert Whitman?"

"Yes, sir."

"I'm Sergeant Victor Dillion. I'm a psychiatrist, sociologist, and criminal profiler."

Robbie just stared.

"Are your parents Robert Andrew Whitman and Jenna Elizabeth Teliaford-Whitman?"

"Yes, sir."

"You have a sister? Rebecca Jenna Whitman, who is disabled?"

"Yes, sir."

"Your address is 13244 East Spring Creek Lane in Bellevue Heights?"

"Yes, sir."

"So, tell me, Robert, why were you with your friends tonight?"

"We went to the beach to watch the meteor shower."

"You were at the beach at one in the morning?"

"Yes, sir."

"Why?"

Robbie gave the man an incredulous look. "I just told you: to watch the meteor shower."

"So, you did. Who is Maximilian Bonnefield to you?"

"Uncle Max? He's like my uncle." Robbie knew some attitude was starting to creep into his tone. He made an effort to swallow it. No sense jumping the guy before he got as much information as he could.

"He is *like* your uncle, or he *is* your uncle?" Sergeant Dillion was making notes as they spoke.

"Well, we're not related if that's what you mean. He's Carrie's real uncle and my adopted uncle."

"How's the water?"

Robbie blinked at the sudden change in topic. "Wet."

"Do you want a soda instead?"

"Can I?" Robbie leaned forward, bouncing in his seat a bit. He loved soda.

"Of course."

Robbie leaned back again; there was something wrong with the psychologist's smile. It was wide and toothy, reminiscent of a vampire. Robbie found himself starting to become a little afraid. The guy was more than creepy—he was right out of a late-night horror movie. Sergeant

Dillion stood up suddenly and exited the room, but Robbie barely had time to sigh with relief before he returned with a glass of soda, ice bobbing around inside. He placed it in front of Robbie, who was distracted by a ring he was wearing. It was gold and black, with a sword and shield symbol on one side and an emerald on top. The man sat back down, the creepy smile plastered on his face again. Robbie looked away, feeling awkward.

"Drink your soda, Robbie. It's okay. It's not poisoned." Sergeant Dillion watched him intently.

Robbie made eye contact again, distrustful. His mind whirled. *Who says things like that? People who poison things, that's who.* Robbie stared at the glass, not reaching for it.

The officer pushed the glass of soda closer to Robbie. "Drink," he insisted.

Robbie decided to hell with it. He was going to show this guy that he wasn't afraid. He wasn't afraid to take a sip of poisoned soda while possibly under arrest by the military and facing no less than three years of being grounded when his parents inevitably found out. This just may be his last soda ever. He took a sip, surprised it was good. He drank a little more. If there was poison, he couldn't taste it. He shrugged, thinking *here goes nothing*, and downed the whole glass. "Where are my friends?"

"Oh, you mean the little girls and that odd fellow, Maximilian?" Sergeant Dillion gave another toothy smile.

"No, the elephant and the dragon!" Robbie was starting to lose his patience.

"Well, well, get some sugar in you, and you get feisty."

"Listen, it's been a long night, I'm tired, the town is frozen solid, and I spent about ten minutes on the craziest ride of my life. I'd like to get home, take a shower, and go to bed, so I can go to school tomorrow." Robbie tried to look stern.

"Well, this is a dilemma. The entire town is frozen solid, except for four people. You, the girls, and the spaceman."

"Spaceman? You mean Uncle Max?" Robbie blinked.

"Once you've been to space, you can be called a spaceman. I assume."

"Uncle Max has been to *space*?" Robbie didn't want the man with all the teeth to know he knew Uncle Max had indeed been to space.

"Oh, very much so. In fact, we owe him a great bit of gratitude for saving us from the aliens so many years ago."

"Are you joking?" Robbie eyed the man carefully, looking for signs of insanity. Well, more signs anyway. He needed to know if this man knew or not.

Sergeant Dillion went back to staring for a moment, not saying anything. Robbie was starting to get very uncomfortable again. Finally, Sergeant Dillion took a deep breath and jotted down a few notes before looking back up at Robbie. "Another soda perhaps?"

"Yes, please. And cookies."

"I'll see what I can do," Sergeant Dillon said. Robbie brightened.

Sergeant Dillion exited again, and this time, as soon as he was gone, Robbie sprang from his chair and started looking for an alternative way out. He tried pulling the bottom of the tent up, but it was heavy and made of thick canvas. Robbie pulled his trusty TAC survival knife out of his boot and was about to cut his way through just as Sergeant Dillion returned. Robbie turned quickly, stashed his knife away, and pretended to have just been stretching his legs. It was going to be a long night.

CHAPTER 15

Max was sitting in front of four high-ranking military officials, all heroes of one sort or another. He didn't know all of them, but he did recognize some of the men were decorated with a rather unique medal, one he also possessed Their chests were decorated in medals. The oldest, sitting at the table, was, like Max himself, a space hero. He had also participated in the galactic battle for Earth so many years ago and was also sworn to secrecy. They have enough problems as it was. The last thing they needed was for the entire planet to know about space aliens and intergalactic wars. But Max and the officer now charged with questioning him, Colonel Henry Alexander Roberts, knew the truth, along with a select group of military and government officials. Including the President of the United States.

"Maximilian Bonnefield, we meet again." Colonel Roberts' stare was piercing.

Max nodded. "It seems so."

"You want to explain what is happening?"

"An alien artifact crash landed, turning this town to ice; can't pick it up, can't touch it, because it turns everything to ice," Max summed up the situation.

"We learned that the hard way." Colonel Roberts rubbed a hand across his wan, lined face. He kept yawning and his eyelids looked heavy. "How can we stop this?"

"I was in the middle of working that out when your MPs decided to bring us in," Max said.

"We've tried everything just short of a nuclear explosion," another of the men contributed.

Max shook his head. "Honestly, I don't know. I've never encountered a device like this before. I need to get a closer look to come up with any answers."

"We are flying in a team of scientists from Washington to take a look at it Max looked over to see a man in a nice black suit with a black tie.

"Listen here..." Max waited for a name.

"Agent Polinsky," the agent said.

"... Agent Polinksy, you can fly in a hundred scientists; they're not going to figure it out any time soon." Max narrowed his eyes. "And, in the meantime, we have an entire town of people who need to become unfrozen immediately."

"Well, as in all cases like this, the people are the least of our worries. We must learn more about the artifact and discover its possibilities." The agent leaned back, looking for all the world like he had just made some kind of profound announcement.

Max was not impressed. "Like how you can manipulate it to use as a weapon?"

The room fell silent for a moment. Colonel Roberts at least looked a bit apologetic. He knew the stakes, but he had to play the game if he wanted to keep his position. Right now, that meant toeing the party line, so to speak. "We understand we owe you a lot of gratitude, but this situation is out of your hands. We will have to wait until our team of scientists arrives before we can proceed. Unfortunately, that means keeping you and the children in custody."

"If you let the people of the town sit on ice for much longer it might cost them their lives. Let the children go and I'll work with you to uncover how the artifact works," Max pleaded softly. He knew if he could get TAC out of custody, they could come up with something.

"You said it yourself: we can bring in a hundred scientists and it won't matter. Why would you be any different?" Agent Polinsky was sneering at him again. Max decided he really didn't like that guy. At all.

He knew Agent Polinsky was likely with the Alien Intelligence Agency, and he badly wished he had the wrist communicator they had taken away from him. In fact, unlike the kids, they took all of his devices; they knew he was a threat. He needed a plan, so he gave them a big smile. "I might have an idea."

"Continue." Colonel Roberts tapped a pen on the table.

"We picked up a ruby that was also unaffected by the ice. It might be worth looking at," Max said.

"A ruby? Why would that work?" Agent Polinksy just kept barging into the conversation. Colonel Roberts started to look as annoyed as Max felt.

"When the artifact landed and started freezing everything, the ruby was the only thing left unfrozen. I found it on the ground, unharmed." Max spoke slowly, enunciating each word carefully. Agent Polinksy clearly needed his hand held to get to the point.

"It didn't freeze?" Colonel Roberts jumped back in.

"It didn't even get cold. It was like the ice avoided it." Max let his voice return to normal.

"Where is it now?" Colonel Roberts made a few quick notes on a yellow legal pad.

"Your men probably locked it up with the rest of my stuff. Which, by the way, I will want back."

"You'll get your stuff back once we see if this ruby really exists or not," Agent Polinsky leaned forward against the table, pointing an accusatory finger at Max.

"Why would I lie about a ruby?" Max was beyond frustrated with this idiot.

"Why not?" Agent Polinsky rolled his eyes.

Max leaned forward himself, getting annoyed beyond his ability to hide it. "Well, for one, I have nothing to hide. I didn't freeze the town!"

"Who knows what you're capable of, Mr. Bonnefield?" The irritating Colonel sneered at him.

Max gave him a toothy smile, too wide for his face smile. He glanced at another officer who had been silent the entire time. This one, he knew, was a war hero and veteran, and had fought bravely in Vietnam, Cuba, and Saudi Arabia. It was this one he addressed his answer to. "The sad truth, Secret Inspector Bonnefield, is that you don't. Isn't that right, dad?"

"Don't I know it, son." Secret Inspector Bonnefield sighed, breaking his silence. They shared a secret smile. "Now, where is my granddaughter?"

CHAPTER 16

Carrie and Leanne sat holding hands as they waited in a large white tent. A female officer stood silently in the corner, keeping watch. She was totally unaware that Carrie and Leanne were talking in code via taps on their palms. They could hold complete conversations about anything and everything using this method, and often did in class. Once, on a mission, Leanne was able to find Carrie in a cave by tapping their code against a wall. Robbie, however, wasn't allowed to use the code anymore. He couldn't spell, and half the time his messages for help came out as declaring various animals were stuck in cheese. The best one was when he said the clown had lost his cheese and there was a dragonfly eating all of the mustard butts.

Right now, they were strategizing on how to get out of the tent and find Robbie and Uncle Max. In the middle of their planning, the tent door swished open, and an older Colonel walked in. Carrie jumped up with a grin. "Grandpa?!"

Her grandfather nodded to the officer who had been guarding them. "You are dismissed."

The woman saluted and exited the tent as Max stepped in. Stepping in directly behind was another man in a black suit and tie. Carrie and Leanne's faces lit up as they ran for him. Max kneeled hugging the girls. "I'm fine. How did they treat you?" Max asked.

"Fine. No one came in or out. We just sat here for like an hour with the quiet lady in the corner," Carrie said. "Where's Robbie?"

"He's with an Alien Intelligence Agent in tent 27." One of the agents who had come in with Max and Grandpa chimed in.

"Why on Earth is he with AIA personnel?" Max asked.

"Good question. I didn't order that." Secret Inspector Bonnefield's eyes narrowed dangerously.

"Under protocol 687 of the intergalactic Earth code and paragraph 79 article 4 section 6.3, any person or persons detained in the event of an alien-terrorist invasion or domestic threat shall be remanded into custody until AIA Agents feel said person is human with no ill intentions," Agent Polinsky cited with a smug grin. Secret Inspector Bonnefield gave him a hard look until the snugness seemed to melt away. "I'll just go acquire him for you, Agent."

"Good idea," Secret Inspector Bonnefield snapped. "Bring him to the mess hall, I'm sure everyone is hungry."

Bonnefield led them out of the tent. They walked through a winding series of tents, laid out like a city block, until Carrie stopped in her tracks. Leanne slammed into her. "What's wrong?" Leanne asked.

"Look!" Carrie said in a whisper. She pointed between the tents to where two men were unloading the still-frozen form of the man from the bed of a truck. It was the man from the beach... the one Carrie was now more certain than ever had been in Mexico as well. The girls shared a look, both knowing this was probably not good news.

"Let's get a closer look." Carrie taking Leanne by her hand. Carrie and Leanne crouched down a little, sneaking off to get a closer look. They passed a tent with a huge video array inside. Carrie was in awe of all the technology. Leanne stared at a monitor that had a view of the earth on it. Before she could say anything, Carrie pulled her by her shoulder, and they continued to move quietly through the tents.

They had made their way pretty close to the scientists escorting the human ice cube on the stretcher when it fell off the top and slammed into the ground. The man was now on his head in the mud, but he was starring right at Carrie. *It is the man from Mexico.* Carrie screamed a little, and they bolted back the way they came.

They quickly caught up to the rest of the group at the mess tent, which was one of the largest in camp. There were at least fifty tables set up with soldiers eating, laughing, talking, playing cards, and relaxing. Everything came to a screeching halt as Secret Inspector Bonnefield walked in. Almost in sync, everyone stood up and saluted him, standing at attention until he waved them down.

The kids got to go to the front of the line and were given all the food they wanted, piled high on their plates. They were all starving, so they sat down with overflowing plates, ready to dig into the huge pile of mashed potatoes, cranberry sauce, large piece of fried chicken, three chocolate chip cookies, and even some broccoli, which Robbie would call *Trees of Mordor.* As they got settled, Robbie was escorted into the room by a strange man. Robbie ran to the table, and Carrie and Leanne got up and hugged him hard. He looked around. "What is going on?"

"Robbie, meet my grandfather, Secretary of Defense and Secret Inspector Theodore Bonnefield," Carrie said. "And that's Colonel Henry Alexander Roberts."

Robbie blinked, then saluted, getting smiles and salutes from both men. He knew the name Henry Alexander Roberts—Max had spoken very highly of him on more than one occasion. Robbie had also read his book entitled *Article 42: The Real Answer* about the possibility of alien life, and what the government was trying to do to make sure everyone got along. "Colonel Roberts, your book was amazing," he managed to stutter, awestruck.

"Thank you, young man." Colonel Roberts smiled again.

Robbie spent another moment basking. One of his heroes knew who he was! Then he looked down at all the food, frowning. "Gross! Trees of Mordor?"

"Please help yourself, Robbie." Secret Inspector Bonnefield pointed toward the buffet. Robbie wasted no time complying. He was starving and had his eye on some meatloaf.

CHAPTER 17

The room was buzzing with hair dryers. Ten soldiers wielding two hair dryers in each hand attempted to thaw Sir Oliver Hedgestone and his assistant from the ice. It was slow-going, but it seemed to be working. The room, however, was nearing 110 degrees. Commander Collins walked in and walked right back out again. "Holy Hot Pocket! It's like a Greek sauna in there."

He motioned to the captain who was in charge of Operation Thaw. "Come and get me once they are de-iced. I'll be in my tent."

Before he could take more than a few steps, however, a young private came running up. "Sir, there is an issue."

"What kind of issue?" Commander Collins narrowed his eyes.

"Well ... sir ... it seems the four suspects have been released."

"What?" The private fidgeted a bit as Commander Collins' voice went flat. "Well ... sir, Secret Inspector Bonnefield and the AIA are in the mess tent eating with them now."

Commander Collins started to turn purple.

"And, uh, that's not all, sir. Apparently, they are related to him in some capacity."

"And what *capacity* would that be?"

Swallowing hard, the private took a few tries to get his voice working again. "One of the children seems to be his grandchild and the strange crazy guy is well ... his son, sir."

Commander Collins just stared at him for a long moment, making the private sweat. "Very well. Thank you, Private. You are dismissed."

Collins made his way back to his own tent. He needed to figure out what this meant to their operations. As he flipped the light on, he suddenly realized he wasn't alone. Two AIA agents were sitting in his chairs. "Ah, Commander Collins. We have many things to discuss. I am agent Coopee, and this is my partner, Agent Lasko."

Commander Collins looked them over. Coopee was thin, balding, and overly pale. Lasko was shorter, thicker, and blonde. "Do we now?" Commander Collins pulled out a fat cigar from his pocket, lighting it up and motioning for the agents to start talking.

"We have heard that you are a man who can get things done. There is a man named Maximilian Bonnefield currently in your camp. He causes problems with our agency and its credibility," Agent Coopee said evenly, not appearing to be bothered by the smoke being blown his way.

"Can I assume he is also the son of Secret Inspector Bonnefield, the Secretary of Defense for the United States?" Commander Collins smirked at them, pleased he could show off that he was informed as well.

Agent Coopee nodded, a small smile forming.

"And what is it you would like me to help with, exactly?"

"We would like you to ... take care of the problem."

"Assassinate him?" Commander Collins asked flatly.

"That's such an ugly word. We would like to remove the threat. We are willing to make some ... necessary adjustments for you as compensation for your help."

"Necessary adjustments?"

"You are a very capable officer—you should have command of your own base. Which would, of course, come with a very dignified increase in pay. Perhaps a comprehensive retirement package to look forward to once you find you are ready to leave this life behind. For example." Agent Coopee gave him another lip locked smile.

Commander Collins snorted. "I've been in the military far too long to know when I'm getting the fat end of a short stick."

The agents looked at each other for a long moment, then Coopee handed Collins a folder. Inside was a picture of his oldest son, Freddy, along with a recommendation letter to Harvard University from the President of the United States. "What is this?" Collins asked.

"Just another example of how we can help you, Sergeant. Your entire family could have a very comfortable, profitable life. All in exchange for one simple task."

He stared at the folder for a long moment before a wicked smile grew. "Where do I sign?"

"No signatures required, Sergeant. The moment Maximilian Bonnefield ceases to be a problem, you will find yourself—and your family—moving up in life."

"How do I know you won't back out of the deal?" Commander Collins tossed the folder on the table and gave the agents another hard look.

"You have our word. Your son will go to Harvard on a football scholarship. From there, he will find himself recruited to the NFL team of his choice. You will find your promotion and reassignment paperwork immediately being processed. I think you will find yourself on, as they say, easy street." Agent Coopee stood up, holding out a hand, and the two shook firmly.

"Gentleman, Mr. Bonnefield will be ... *retired* ... before the ink dries on the scholarship paperwork."

"We are counting on you, Commander Collins. Do not let the AIA down."

CHAPTER 18

The helipad was chaotic as Max, Carrie, Leanne, and Robbie watched Secret Inspector Bonnefield and his team—including Colonel Roberts—depart. Max waved and gave everyone a hearty smile and thumbs up, but, inwardly, he was concerned. There were a lot of men still in camp who he knew would actively work against them, and with the Secretary of Defense no longer in residence, it opened up the door to trouble.

Speaking of which, Max turned to see several agents he knew wanted him out of the picture. Permanently, if they could find a way to manage it. He immediately put himself between the children and the agents. Max knew these men hated him because of the Galactic Hero he was. They too were in the battle above earth but never prestige to their highest positions and they blame him. "Agent Coopee, Agent Lasko, Agent Dillion, I didn't realize you were on location," he said coolly.

"We are here for the rather unusual ruby you seem to have ... acquired, Mr. Bonnefield." Agent Coopee had always struck him as slimy. Max strongly suspected the man was not what he pretended to be, but thus far he hadn't managed to uncover any evidence.

For now, though, he would play along. It wasn't just his own well-being he needed to worry about, but the children and an entire town of frozen people. "Take me to my stuff and you'll get it."

"Of course. Right this way."

The agents led them to another tent full of boxes and crates. someone had written "Property of the US Government—Carrie Calusa" on several of the boxes. Carrie yelped, "That's my stuff! The government doesn't own my things!" She ran over and started to open one of the boxes. Agent Lasko grabbed her arm, wrenching her back so hard that it made her cry out.

Max smacked the agent's hand off of Carrie, spinning the man's arm behind his back before he could react. "Don't ever touch her again, or I'll rip this chicken bone you call an arm off and use it as a croquet mallet." Max rarely dropped his affable, oddball persona, but no one was going to hurt his charges. No one.

Agent Coopee placed his hand on Max's shoulder. "Please let go of the government official you are currently assaulting."

"Assaulting! That bozo nearly broke my arm!" Carrie sniffed.

Robbie leaped forward to help Max, his fists clenched tight.

"You know, little children can be locked up, too. And lost forever. Do you want to be placed in a home for young boys?" Agent Coopee sneered.

"No," Robbie said, looking away. For the first time in a long while, he was frightened. He didn't know what these men were up to. He didn't trust any of them, and they had the means to make them all disappear. He wished this case involved chasing ancient warriors through the jungle. Or even better: Bigfoot or the Loch Ness Monster. Robbie had faced all of those with less fear than he had now. Well, maybe not Nessie. That was a huge monster, and he's pretty sure none of Team Adventure Club will ever be allowed back into Scotland. Ever.

Max let the agent go and stepped back, looking down at Robbie. He was furious the agent had scared him. Max gave the agent a hard look but didn't say anything. He found his box and took his stuff back, then found all of the boxes with the children's names on them. His movements slow and deliberate, he pulled out their belongings and handed them out, daring any of the agents to stop him. None of them moved.

As a team, all three put on their TAC COMs and brought them back online. "Welcome Team. Synchronization is complete. Heartbeats are slightly elevated but within normal parameters. Proceed normally," the computer chirped.

The agents looked impressed, despite themselves. "What is that you have there?" Agent Coopee asked.

"Intellectual property, Agent Coopee. Back off." Max gave him a deep dimpled sarcastic smile.

"That looks like alien technology to me, Mr. Bonnefield." Agent Dillion moved closer to get a better look.

"It also shoots lasers if you really want to find out," Max said, pointing his device at them.

"We are all on the same side." Agent Dillion reminded him, though he hadn't taken his eyes off of the TAC COMs.

"Are we?" Leanne asked. She was usually the quiet one, but if she needed to say something, she did. The agents looked at her, arms folded as she waited for an answer. There was none. "That's what I thought."

Agent Coopee changed the subject. "The ruby? Where is it?"

Max gave a sly smile and reached over, pulling it out of the agent's own pocket. When he had been in the interrogation room, he held the ruby in his hand, cloaked until he was addressed by Agent Coopee. It had been easy to slip it into his pocket. The agent was so distracted by his own ego he hadn't felt it happen.

With a hard look, Agent Coopee reached for it. Max snatched it back, keeping it just out of reach. "Give me the ruby, Mr. Bonnefield. Now."

"I can carry it to wherever you want to use it," Max smirked.

"We will be taking it to our lab," Agent Coopee said. "I am afraid you are not allowed on the premises."

Agent Lasko gave a meaningful look at the children, who were staring in awe at Max. Max understood Lasko's threat; he wasn't willing to risk the children's safety.

Just as he was about to hand it over, Commander Collins burst in with Sir Oliver

Hedgestone. "There they are! Team Adventure Club! They stole my ruby!"

Carrie looked at Leanne and huffed. "Oh great! Here we go again."

"I think we should run," Robbie added.

CHAPTER 19

They fell out of the tent in a jumble. Robbie tripped over Carrie, Carrie tripped over Leanne, and Uncle Max pushed all of them out as fast as he could. They quickly regained their footing and moved fast, dodging soldiers trying to grab them like they had been born for it.

They managed to make it clear of the tents, but the number of people chasing them was only increasing. Max and Robbie had gotten ahead of the girls, but Leanne changed course without warning. Carrie stumbled trying not to run into her, but she quickly caught back up. "Leanne! Where are you going? We have to get out of here!"

She wordlessly pointed, and Carrie's eyes widened as she realized where they were heading.

Robbie and Max, meanwhile, were the soldiers' main targets, who had managed to outflank them. They were surrounded. "You're not going any farther," one of the soldiers announced with a nasty smile.

Carrie and Leanne, forgotten for the moment, boarded the empty and unguarded helicopter. "Keep your head down," Carrie said as they ducked inside. "They'll never look for us if we're hiding in here."

"Hiding? I'm going to fly this thing." Leanne moved to the pilot's seat, flipping switches on the console

"Wait. What?" Carrie squeaked.

"Yeah, this is an AC-456 Bridgeport F-lass." Leanne mumbled, paying more attention to what she was doing than to Carrie.

"So?" Carrie was confused.

"Remember, the Island of Robot Monkeys? This is what I flew to get us out of the volcano."

"If you recall, I was blind from the laser rockets at the time," Carrie noted.

"Oh yeah. Well, this is what I used. It's pretty simple to fly, actually." Leanne flipped a few more switches, and the chopper came to life. The rotors turned slowly.

"Kick the tires and light some fires!" Carrie said, sliding into the co-pilot seat. Leanne chuckled at the phrase.

"Maybe, start the motor and spin those rotors," Leanne said.

"I'll just assume you know how to fly a chopper," Carrie said, strapping herself in.

"I had to learn pretty quickly. I kind of made the rest up as I went along."

"Wait, so you flew us home in a chopper you didn't know how to fly?" Carrie hissed.

"I got the hang of it." Leanne shrugged and strapped on a flight helmet. "Please remain seated during our flight and keep your tray table and seat in the upright and locked position."

Carrie raised an eyebrow.

"In other words, strap in and hold on," Leanne said, flipping her visor down. The helicopter lifted off just as the soldiers realized one of their own wasn't flying. The helicopter circled around to where Robbie and Max were being ordered to lay on the ground with their hands behind their heads. Leanne flipped on the helicopter's bright spotlight. It lit up the area, making everyone blink.

"Step away from the prisoners." Carrie's voice came over the speaker system. The soldier who had been getting ready to cuff Max and Robbie looked up.

Once she was sure she had his attention, Leanne engaged the weapons system. Four rockets dropped down into launch position, aimed squarely at the group on the ground. After a long pause, the soldiers all laid their guns on the ground, putting their own hands behind their heads. Uncle Max and Robbie scrambled back to their feet and ran over to where Carrie had dropped down a rope ladder. "Hurry up and get in!" she shouted, leaning out of the door.

"Smell ya' later, suckers!" Leanne shouted as both the boys scrambled on board. Leanne took them up and out of harm's way. They all got strapped into the seats, pulling on helmets, and making sure the communication system was up and running. The camp disappeared over the horizon,

"We need to move fast. I think I have a way to configure this Ruby into a mechanism that will let us contain the sphere safely," Uncle Max said as soon as their microphones were all online. "Head to my cabin in the Rockies."

Thirty-three minutes later, Leanne carefully set the helicopter down in a clearing behind the cabin. She just hoped they had time to finish whatever they were doing here before someone flew overhead and noticed a large, stolen military-grade machine where one should not be.

Inside, they got a variety of snacks and headed down into the basement, where a state-of-the-art workshop and command center was hidden. "How can we stop this thing from freezing everything?" Carrie asked.

Uncle Max walked over to a table, placing both hands on the surface to activate the sensors. A virtual keyboard appeared, and he quickly started inputting information. A box came out from inside of the table, and he carefully put the ruby inside. Immediately, information started scrolling across all the screens as the gem was analyzed down to its molecular level.

"The ruby is the most stable gem, right? That means it is Ai_2o_3, which means there's aluminum in its makeup. Aluminum doesn't freeze, so that must be the reason it wasn't affected." He paused, an odd look on his face. "Wait! Silk!" He spent several more minutes typing and muttering to himself as he ran more tests and scenarios. "Okay. I think I've got it!" He did a little dance.

Carrie rolled her eyes at him. "Great, how?"

"So, a diamond has a Mohs scale—which is used to measure the hardness of different minerals—of 10, and the ruby rates a 9. The aluminum ions replaced the chromium ions, and that's why rubies are red. There's more science to that, but that's the short version. What's important is that because of those properties, rubies were used to make the first lasers in the 1960s by Theodore Maiman. And I can use it to make a box to contain the UFO!"

Uncle Max raised the box and took out the ruby, holding it up to the light. He brought it to a laser cutter, carefully inputting the dimensions he would need. He stopped several times, measuring the air with his hands before glancing back at Carrie. "You think the UFO was about this big?"

Carrie shook her head. "I don't know."

Max made a face, continuing to try to estimate the size with his hands. "We can't make a mistake on this. If the ruby container is too small, it won't fit, but if we go too big, we may not have enough ruby. I hope I'm right."

He started typing again, but Carrie suddenly shouted, making everyone jump. "Wait! I have an idea of how we can be sure!" She looked up at the lights. She thought back to the moment when she had seen the sphere while they were at the military camp. She hadn't really paid attention at the time because there was so much happening, but she had seen the exact dimensions, an aftereffect of Robbie's calculating glasses. She tried hard to picture exactly what she had seen, the numbers scrolling across her vision. The numbers hit her like a wave, making her stumble and fall to the floor.

"Carrie! Are you okay?" Uncle Max rushed to her side.

"I know the answer." She beamed at him. "The length of the sphere is two and three eighth inches, the width is three and one eighth inches, and the height is three and one eighths of an inch!"

"Are you sure?" Uncle Max paused in his quest to look her over for injuries.

"Of course, she's sure!" Robbie pumped his fist in the air. "My Math Glasses have been burned into her retinas. And you're welcome for that!"

Uncle Max rose and went to put the numbers into the computer. The machine came to life, and they watched as the laser cut the ruby. It cut four sides, then the bottom, and then the top, before applying some of Max's special adhesive to connect it all together. It was the most expensive jewelry box ever made.

Max carefully picked it up and stowed it in his bag. "Let's go get us an asteroid."

"It's a U.F.O." Robbie said.

"Meteorite? Isn't it?" Leanne starred at all of them.

"Sphere. It's like a sphere. Actually, it's a missile from an alien enemy," Carrie said.

"Bomb?" Uncle Max chined in. "Let's just go with U.F.O." They all nodded.

"Team Adventure Club, go!" Carrie shouted, putting her hand out.

Robbie, Leanne, and Max followed suit. "TEAM ADVENTURE CLUB!" they shouted in unison.

"Well, this sounds like a cheerleading club to me," Agent Coopee smirked. They all whirled around to see him standing on the stairs.

"Poop," Carrie sighed.

"And what exactly are you up to down here? Very nice secret lair by the way."

Agent Coopee stepped, further in brandishing his weapon. Which look like a ray gun.

"Is that a ray gun?" Robbie excitedly yelp.

Everyone looked at him for a moment. "No this is stun gun. I'm not a monster." Agent Coopee said.

"But you'll still stun us into incapacitation. Nice guy." Carrie said.

Max was glad he had already stowed the box. "Well, we were hiding until you found us," he pointed out.

"You do realize the helicopter you stole has a GPS tracker on it," Agent Coopee remarked coolly.

"Just bring them up here!" Agent Lasko's voice drifted down the stairs.

"You heard 'em. Move!"

The gang walked up the stairs with Uncle Max bringing up the rear. In the living room, four soldiers dressed in black stood with guns drawn. They pointed them at Max and the kids.

"You can't keep us here. We're children! You have to be violating some mandate or law or something!" Carrie shouted.

Agent Coopee grabbed her by the chin and squeezed. "You've got a big mouth for such a small girl. If you don't want to end up with it broken, you might want learn to keep it shut."

Uncle Max narrowed his eyes. "I warned you that if you touched or harmed any of these children, I would retaliate. You've just crossed my line."

"What are you going to do about it?" Agent Coopee mocked him, squeezing a little harder. Carrie whimpered.

In one fluid movement, Uncle Max spun around and picked up the nearest table lamp, smashing it across Agent Coopee's head. He grabbed Carrie and pushed her behind him where she would be safe. One of the soldiers started to bring his gun around, but Max kicked out, catching him across the stomach. Then, he landed a right hook across his face. Finally, Max grabbed his arm and swung him around and down; the guy's head struck the coffee table, and he went limp.

"Bolos!" Leanne shouted.

Robbie and Carrie reached into a pocket on their belts and pulled out a tube. They put one end on their TAC COM and loaded them like muskets from the Civil War.

Uncle Max had been busy dealing with the rest of the soldiers. He pulled the only one still conscious to his feet, spinning him around and putting him in a headlock. "We are only trying to help!" he said to Agent Coopee as he slammed the guy to the floor.

"Then perhaps you should end this charade!" Agent Coopee pulled out a gun of his own.

Robbie turned to fire, but Agent Lasko threw a vase at him, and knocked him out cold. Carrie and Leanne hit the Agents with the bolos. It wrapped them both up like turkeys, forcing their arms and legs tightly against their bodies. "Son of a—," Agent Coopee swore as he dropped the gun and tumbled to the floor.

The cabin door flung open to reveal Sir Oliver Hedgestone. He looked less frozen and more put together than the last time they had seen him. It was obvious he was very, very angry. His entire forehead was bright red as well as his cheeks and the tip of his nose. He clenched his teeth hard.

"Give me the ruby!" His voice was soft, but it sent chills up everyone's spines.

Max patted his pockets and looked confused. "What ruby? I haven't seen any ruby."

"This is not a game you wish to play. Hand it over, or you and these ... children ... will find yourselves in very, shall we say, unpleasant circumstances."

Max glanced at Carrie, trying to wordlessly will her to run. But Carrie wasn't going anywhere. She knew if she left and something happened, she would never forgive herself. Suddenly, she burst into tears. "Stop, I just want to go home!"

It was a little overdramatic, she could admit, but it was effective. Sir Oliver Hedgestone actually looked startled. Leanne knelt next to Robbie, trying to get him to wake up. She caught Carrie's eye and realized what was going on. She put both hands over her face and started to sob, too.

Sir Oliver Hedgestone took a deep breath before pulling out a small gun, pointing it right at Uncle Max. "Give me the ruby or your dear uncle is going to suffer."

Both girls stopped crying and gave him identical hard looks. "Don't you do anything stupid, Baldy," Leanne warned.

"Give me the ruby, and I'll be on my way. You and the military can work out your ... issues ... without my interference."

Uncle Max had absently scraped the dust from the cutting into his pocket earlier, and now he got as much of a handful as he could. When Sir Oliver Hedgestone's attention was on Carrie, Max tossed the ruby dust directly into his face. The powder shimmered like a beautiful waterfall of red, making him back up suddenly and drop the gun.

"My eyes!" Sir Oliver Hedgestone screamed.

"Run!" Uncle Max yelled, grabbing Robbie from the floor as he darted past. They ran back to the helicopter they had stolen, throwing on helmets as Leanne got the motors started back up. "GO! GO! GO!"

Leanne did just that, pulling back on the joystick. The helicopter lifted off the ground and into the air.

CHAPTER 20

The whirling of the blades created a wonderful breeze across Robbie's face. He imagined that he was in a field somewhere enjoying the cool summer day. He could hear laughter in the distance, and he thought of hot dogs and cotton candy. Then he opened his eyes and sighed. The smell of gasoline and rubber filled his nostrils, and the sound of metal rattling on the helicopter brought him right back to present moment.

"You okay?" Uncle Max asked from his seat on the opposite bench.

Robbie looked out over the dark forest with city lights winking in the distance. In the cockpit, he could see Leanne piloting and Carrie's head bent over her TAC COM. Uncle Max's hair rustled like seaweed in the turbulent air.

"Robbie?" Uncle Max repeated.

He forced a weak smile. "I'm fine. My head just hurts."

"That's because it was hit with a 5000-year-old vase. A priceless, one-of-a-kind Egyptian relic. But, you know, whatever," Uncle Max patted his shoulder gingerly.

"Well, as long as I'm fine, right?" Robbie managed a grin.

"He probably has a concussion," Leanne added through the microphone.

"Oh, yeah. Much better."

Robbie squinted at Uncle Max for a moment until the vision of two Uncle Maxes became one.

"It was 5000 years old, Robbie!" Uncle Max yelled.

"I didn't smash it with my face on purpose!"

They were interrupted by Carrie as she plopped onto the bench next to Max. She had been plotting their course. "These coordinates say we're only about a minute away from the GAST Center."

"GAST Center?" Robbie blinked, dragging his mind back on target.

"The Galactic Assembly for Science and Technology Center, our next destination." Uncle Max rubbed a hand across his face.

Leanne landed them in an open field that contained only a small concrete hatch door in the ground at its center. "Is that it?" she called.

Uncle Max turned, putting half his body out of the wide opening of the helicopter to get a better look at the field.

"That's it!" Uncle Max hopped out, the ground squelching. The mud was up past his ankles. He picked up one foot and gave it a horrified stare.

Robbie, Leanne, and Carrie followed, all finding themselves in mud up to their knees. Carrie looked as disgusted as Uncle Max while Robbie just shrugged it off. Leanne grinned. "Now, this is an adventure!" she remarked.

At the door, Uncle Max pulled out a large metallic key. It was long, and square. In the center of the door, there were two blue lights, and a thumbprint identifier. When Max put the key in the lock, the lights turned green, and the scanner verified his identity.

"Why are we here?" Robbie leaned forward to watch with interest.

"We need the largest magnifying glass known to man," Uncle Max grunted as he pulled the heavy door open.

Inside, the lights flickered on as they walked down the narrow concrete corridor. From the other side, lights flickered on as a group came to greet them. As they approached, it was easy to make out that one of them was a scientist with three guards flanking her. Robbie was awestruck at her beauty: long curly black hair, big bright blue eyes only accentuated by her large glasses, and her skin looked like warm root beer. Uncle Max put his hand out to shake, but she smacked him across the face instead.

"I haven't heard from you in three months!" She seemed shaken, but quickly regained her composure when she noticed the kids. "Who are these little darlings?"

"Hello, Isabelle," Max said, rubbing his cheek. "This is my niece Carrie, and her friends Leanne and Robbie. Who are basically like family."

"Why on Earth have you brought children to the GAST Center?" Isabelle hissed through her teeth, her smile brittle.

"Who is this?" Carrie said with a smile.

"Kids, meet Isabelle Chaudhuri, the foremost expert on Exterior Planet Defense."

All the kids smiled.

"Nice to meet you," Isabelle said.

"Are you two dating?" Carrie asked.

Both Isabelle and Uncle Max looked at each other with wide eyes.

"We need the YOLO Telescope," Max said, breaking the awkward moment.

Isabelle raised an eyebrow. "Why? Are you showing them the surface of Jupiter?"

"No, no. We need to reposition it toward Earth, on Bellevue Heights specifically. I'll fill you in on the way," Max said.

They continued down the corridor to yet another large metal door. Isabelle ushered them inside, and all three kids stopped and stared. It was huge. Carrie couldn't believe that all of this was underground. The massive chamber looked like a control room for NASA with tons of people milling around in lab coats and suits. It seemed like everyone knew Uncle Max.

Isabelle grabbed Max, pulling him aside. "Why haven't you called me?"

"I was working. I just got back a few days ago only to have my entire hometown frozen solid." He sighed.

"You don't think we're aware of the projectile that froze your town?" Isabelle asked. She pressed a button, and the monitors all switched to show different angles of Bellevue Heights.

On one screen, Carrie watched as the soldiers tried to figure out ways to pick up the UFO. On another, Carrie spotted a caravan of SUVs pulling up. On the side of each of the three SUVs, Hedgestone Corp was written in a boxed military font. Sir Oliver Hedgestone exited one of them, looking worse for wear, but still elegant and angry. "Uh, guys?"

Everyone came over to look. Isabelle pressed a few buttons and the screen zoomed in, analyzing his face. A moment later, a full bio appeared, following him as he walked into the camp. "'That is Sir Oliver Hedgestone, a billionaire, explorer and extortionist. He's ruthless and will stop at nothing until he has what he wants,'" Isabelle read aloud.

"Oh, we know him!" Carrie made a face.

"You do?" Isabelle asked.

"Yeah, we've met him a few times, but we've never been properly introduced. I think Uncle Max may have blinded him," Carrie said.

"How?" Isabelle glanced over at Max, who was trying to look innocent.

"Ruby dust," Carrie beamed.

"Just be careful and don't cross him. He's bad news, and you don't need him as an enemy." Isabelle glanced back at the screen, shaking her head.

Transfixed, the group watched the screens. Suddenly, Uncle Max clapped his hands, making everyone jump. "Okay. Let's get \to the YOLO telescope."

"You can't just *go* to the Yellers Outer-Space Light Observer Telescope, Max." Isabelle looked cross again. "Not without the proper clearance."

Max pulled out an ID card that stated he has Top Secret clearance. Isabelle looked at it for a long moment before handing it back. She shook her head, but it was obvious she was ready to admit defeat. "Okay then, let's go."

Isabelle pulled Uncle Max aside, grabbing his face with both hands. "Why haven't you called me? I was worried sick. You can't just leave and come back whenever you want. That's not fair to me."

"I'm sorry. I got stuck in a tunnel for like a week and half."

Isabelle looked at him for a long hard moment. "Where?"

"In a tunnel!"

"Where was the tunnel?" she pressured him.

"Underground," Uncle Max said with a cock-sure grin.

"Why?"

"I was in Bolivia, chasing down a rouge group of Pathlorphians, you know? Those teddy bear looking guys from the Vicotorne Galaxy. Any way, they eluded me, and I got stuck. For a week and half. In a tunnel," Uncle Max explained.

"I don't buy it. Mainly because I assume you didn't eat or drink anything for that time and that would mean you would be dead. So," Isabelle said.

"Actually, I lost thirty-nine pounds and that was the only way I was able to squeeze out of the tunnel. So don't *so* me."

"I'm not kissing you yet. So," Isabelle said, walking away.

CHAPTER 21

The doctors laid Sir Oliver Hedgestone on an operating table. He didn't look good. The ruby dust damaged his eyes and the doctors wanted to get it out as fast as they could. It was going to be a long process.

Outside, Colonel Roberts was furious. "Do you mind explaining to me why several military personnel and AIA Agents were chasing a bunch of twelve-year-olds around the state?"

"They are wanted fugitives, sir." Commander Collins refused to back down.

"What on Earth could three twelve-year-olds have done to make you get in the most expensive helicopters we own and try to shoot them out of the sky?"

"Sir, we were also after Maximilian Bonnefield," Commander Collins pointed out.

Colonel Roberts gave him a hard look before turning to Agents Coopee and Lasko. "You two! What are you up to?"

"We are under orders to only speak to Sir Oliver Hedgestone," Agent Coopee said.

Colonel Roberts never took his eyes off them as he gestured toward Commander Collins. "Arrest this man."

Several Military Police standing nearby quickly moved in, handcuffing the officer. "Why are you arresting me?" Commander Collins sputtered.

"For plotting to kill children." Colonel Roberts watched as both agents' faces contorted in surprise before their expressions went blank again. "As for you two, I'm watching."

Colonel Roberts and Secret Inspector Bonnefield, who had stood by watching silently, headed toward the command tent. Agents Coopee and Lasko just looked at each other and smiled.

Colonel Roberts and Secret Inspector Bonnefield walked past the field where soldiers were still freezing themselves. "Someone tell those men to stop trying to pick it up. Look at the fifty other soldiers who are frozen solid—they are not going to succeed," Secret Inspector Bonnefield barked at a passing soldier. The soldier abruptly changed direction to go take care of the problem.

Inside the tent, Commander Collins' handcuffs were removed. "You think they bought the bait?" Colonel Roberts asked, sitting down in one of the chairs.

"I hope so. What kind of mad man puts out a hit on twelve-year-olds?" Commander Collins took another chair, rubbing at his wrists.

"So, we just wait."

"It must have been tempting to go through with taking the deal, knowing your son could have gone to Harvard." Colonel Roberts pushed an open laptop over, giving the sergeant access to their current data.

"Not at all. I explained it to my son, and he and I agreed it wasn't worth the stress of knowing that his only reason for being in school was because I had harmed anyone. Children or otherwise."

"Admirable." Colonel Roberts smiled.

Meanwhile, in the medical tent, the doctors removed the ruby dust from Sir Oliver Hedgestone's eyes. It was a difficult and arduous process, but they finally had to call it. "Okay, wrap up his eyes. I think I've done all I can. We need to Aeroflight him to the nearest hospital. They might be able to do more there." The doctor in charge set down his instruments, looking tired. The nurses jumped into action, preparing the patient for transport and calling for the medical evac.

Agents Lasko and Coopee watched as the medical helicopter was loaded and quickly flew away. They both straightened their ties and made their way to the black SUV waiting for them. As they approached, the SUV's doors opened, and several MPs stepped out followed by Secret Inspector Bonnefield. "Agents." He gave them both a humorless smile. "Soldiers, arrest these men."

"Arrest us? We are AIA Agents." Agent Lasko stood up straighter. "You can't arrest us. We are a branch of the government that answers only to the Executive Administrator for the agency."

"Have you ever met the Executive Administrator of the AIA?" Secret Inspector Bonnefield raised an eyebrow.

"No," Agent Lasko said, but he was cut off before he could say anything more.

"Well, now you can say you have had the pleasure," Secret Inspector Bonnefield said, bowing slightly. He pulled out a silver and gold badge featuring an eagle with spread wings in front of a circular flying saucer and a sunburst. A banner underneath read "The Stars are just the Beginning" in bold lettering.

Both agents went pale. They obediently stuck out their hands and the MPs promptly snapped handcuffs on their wrists. "We were just following orders," Agent Lasko said.

"Yes. From an unsanctioned and non-liable billionaire who is in no way a part of our chain of command." Secret Inspector Bonnefield glared at them. "Get them out of my sight."

CHAPTER 22

Carrie, Leanne, and Robbie were in awe as they stepped into one of the biggest rooms they had ever been in. From floor to ceiling it must have been twenty stories tall, all open. It was currently housing several sleek space shuttles that were more futuristic looking than anything NASA had in their arsenal. Along the sides of the warehouse were catwalks leading completely around the interior of the room. Men and women worked on various parts of the shuttles. A forklift driven by a man in a bright green vest and hard cat zipped by carrying a pallet with a silver piece of metal on it.

"Are these our spaceships?" Carrie asked in a whisper, afraid to raise her voice.

"Yes." Isabelle smiled. "But these are so much better. Come on."

Isabelle ushered them further down the catwalk to an open service elevator. Robbie couldn't stop staring at the shuttles. He really wanted to ride in one. As the elevator descended the four stories to the floor below, Leanne suddenly grabbed Max's hand. Uncle Max didn't know how to react. Was she just scared or was there something more to this? He turned his attention back to the shuttles, letting her squeeze his hand until the elevator touched down.

As they exited the elevator, they were met by a large, muscular man with frosted eyeglasses and an enormous afro. He was wearing a lab coat like the other workers at the facility, but, beneath it, he wore jeans and sneakers, rather than business attire. His sneakers had roller skate attachments, which made him appear to float across the cement floor. Isabelle rolled her eyes at him. "This is Doctor Rafael Williams, our professor of transorbital rotation and engineering."

He spun in a circle and gave Max a high five. "Maximilian, my man! I heard you were in Mexico dealing with some Aztec gold."

"I was, but it's all good now." Max said, going into a complicated handshake with a lot of finger wiggling and palm slapping.

"And who are these fine-looking kids?" Rafael held up a hand for Robbie, who enthusiastically high-fived him as well.

"We're Team Adventure Club!" Carrie said proudly.

"I'll be! The Team Adventure Club? I've heard so much about you. Consider me your biggest fan." He gave them all a huge thumbs up with both hands. "Call me Rafa."

They all introduced themselves, and Rafa shook his head. "Crazy stuff, man. You kids are wild. Gotta watch out for my job!" He grinned at them. "So, what brings you here to this fine establishment?"

Max pointed to the middle shuttle. Rafa spun on his skates a few times. "You want the KRS-1?"

"I need to get to the YOLO and reposition it toward Earth."

Rafa looked at them for a long moment before nodding. "Chance to be part of a TAC mission? Count me in. Let's do this."

Rafa led them to a locker room. On the walls, spacesuits hung in a wide range of colors and patterns. Leanne was immediately drawn to the black ones. "These are the coolest!"

Carrie ran her hand over one of the suits. The material felt strange; it was rubbery and soft but firm at the same time. The elbows and knees had padding already in place, and the shoulders looked as if there was a hard plastic shell over them. There was a small GAST logo on the right side of the chest and a NASA logo on the left. The back had carbon metal running down the center of the spine, with two straps that wrapped around to the front of the suit connecting it to the front chest piece.

They continued past the suits and through a weight room with astronauts running on treadmills and lifting weights. Through a window, Carrie watched as one of them sparred with what she thought was a human—until its head was kicked off. Carrie looked at Robbie with surprised glee. "They have robots!"

"I know! Did you see how he kicked its head off?" Robbie vibrated with excitement.

Uncle Max leaned in, patting them on the shoulders. "You haven't seen anything yet."

CHAPTER 23

The suit was a little small on Uncle Max. He danced around, wiggling his fat until he was finally able to zip it up. It made him look skinnier, he thought, and he admired himself in the full-length mirror. He was proud to be in a flight suit again. It had been far too long since his last foray into space.

Carrie, also wearing a spacesuit, came around the corner. Max grinned at her. "You look awesome!" they said in unison.

Carrie's smile was quickly broken when Leanne walked in, stone-faced. She was furious that she wasn't going to get to go to space. Robbie was happy that he didn't have to leave the Earth's atmosphere today. He wasn't big on heights, and leaving the Earth was getting pretty high. Too high. Being able to see Earth with his own eyes from space was the last thing in his book of Things You Need to Do Before You Die.

"I am so jealous that you get to go into space!" Leanne huffed.

"Leanne, we need you to fly the helicopter back to base so Robbie can grab the UFO and conceal it in the ruby box." Max patted her on the shoulder.

"I know. But..." She moaned, looking at Carrie—and Carrie's spacesuit —with puppy-dog eyes.

"We'd better get going, folks. You have thirty-two minutes to get to the space station and redirect toward Bellevue Heights. After that, you're going to have to wait an entire day," Rafa said as he skated into the locker room.

Uncle Max smiled at Carrie. "Ready?"

The door to the main hangar opened, and they saw the giant ships once again. "Since we have to get you into space rather quickly, we'll take the middle one." Rafa smiled. "It's the fastest out of the three and should get us into space in about five minutes. We'll get to the station in twenty minutes, giving us twelve minutes to work on the positioning of the YOLO."

"Okay, Leanne, get Robbie to the UFO and get it in the box. Then, you need to seal it up tight and put it in another locked box. You have forty-five minutes to get back to Bellevue Heights." Max put both hands on her shoulders, forcing her to refocus on her own important task.

"Thirty-two minutes to go one hundred miles? That's a 187.5 miles an hour. Most military helicopters can maintain an average speed of about 200 miles an hour, so we should be fine." She beamed at him.

"That's what I like to hear!" Uncle Max said, warmly squeezing her shoulders. "No one else can fly a helicopter like you."

Leanne and Robbie watched as the other members of Team Adventure Club loaded into the shuttle. "We'd better move!" Robbie said as the hatch was latched behind them.

The inside of the shuttle was something Max had been longing to see. The console was a solid piece of glass that spanned the entire front. On the glass was an array of holographic dials, buttons, and levers. The windshield contained a heads-up display that matched the glass console. The seats were covered in white leather with orange piping and stitching. The flooring was a soft foam core with a lighted walking path. Max smiled as memory after memory washed over him. "Where do you want me?" he asked Rafa.

"You can pilot, my good man. I'll navigate." Rafa smacked Max on the back, taking his own place.

Max sat in the pilot's seat. He strapped himself in, adjusted the buckles and steering column, and looked over the console before pressing a red button. The console buzzed to life, revealing that the entire thing was a touchscreen. Rafa did the same, booting up the navigation console. Carrie took her seat behind them. As the ship whizzed to life, the seat belts automatically readjusted, squeezing them in tight. Uncle Max grunted, not entirely able to exhale. "They really want you to be safe, huh?"

He could feel the rumble of the engines through the seat. He loved the feeling of the ship coming to life, ready for its journey. He pressed several buttons on the monitor, watching as the giant bay doors opened. Then hydraulics pushed the shuttle up to a forty-five-degree angle. They were ready to launch.

Rafa finished programming their course and grinned at Max. "Here we go!"

The shuttle blasted off so fast that they were 30,000 feet in the air before Carrie could blink. All she could see were clouds whizzing by. She glanced at the altimeter in the center of the console as it passed 51,000 feet. Her eyes grew wide; they were outside the Earth's atmosphere. She could see stars. She was amazed at how beautiful it was.

"Cool, isn't it?" Uncle Max asked.

Carrie couldn't find words. She just nodded with a wide grin and look of wonder in her eyes. She could see the moon up-close, craters and all. It looked totally different up close, far bigger than she ever imagined and so much brighter. And so close. She felt as if she could swim to it and walk around. The sun was still very far away, but she could see that in exquisite detail too. Carrie raised her TAC COM toward the front window and snapped a few pictures. She couldn't wait to show Leanne and Robbie. She did a little dance in her seat. Then she noticed that both Rafa and Uncle Max were also dancing in their seats.

"Woot! Woot! We're in space! We're in space!" they all sang.

Meanwhile, Leanne was pushing her helicopter to its limits. They were flying so fast and so low that Robbie could've reached out and touched the tops of the trees. He tapped on his TAC COM, and It buzzed to life. "Another eight minutes and we'll be there!" he said, examining the GPS readout.

"Good. I can't wait for this night to be over!" Leanne sulked.

"What's wrong with you?" Robbie asked.

"I just … ugh … it's not fair. I'm the pilot! I'm the one who should have gone to space! Carrie doesn't even want to be an astronaut. I do! She's a geologist, not a pilot! I'm the one who should be in space right now," Leanne wailed.

"But you're pushing the very limit with one of the government's super-secret helicopters!" Robbie pointed out.

"I know. I get it. But it's just not fair!"

"Six minutes," Robbie said, his eyes back on the TAC COM.

"Are you even listening to me?"

Robbie rolled his eyes, sorry he had brought it up, but he nodded.

"I love her, Robbie, but sometimes … I mean … graaaah. Right?" She gestured wildly as she complained.

The helicopter dipped to the right and then to the left as Leanne ranted. Robbie grabbed his restraints tightly. The helicopter dipped forward briefly.

"Both hands on the controls there, missy!" Robbie grabbed at his seat as the helicopter shook, going a little white.

"I'm not going to crash. If I can't go to space, I'm going to break a speed record! You can bank on it," she shouted.

CHAPTER 24

The shuttle silently coasted through space. Every once in a while, a thruster would hiss out a long, extended boost of fusion. The space-ship seemed so tiny against the backdrop of the vast universe. The stars reflected off the metal exterior and it was almost as if the ship got lost in the starry blanket of the cosmos.

"We're about three minutes out," Rafa said, looking back at Carrie. "Once we dock with the space station, Harry will meet us. He's already calculated the trajectory of the angle in which we'll need to position the telescope. Max, it's up to you to replace the lens."

"Carrie and I can spacewalk out to the front of the telescope." Max said, tapping the console.

"Wait. a 'spacewalk'?" Carrie blinked.

"Yes. We have to go out to the telescope and flip the lens, so it magnifies the sun's heat. It shouldn't take but a moment," Max shot a smile back at her trying to reassure her.

Carrie gripped the armrests until her knuckles turned white. *Going into space is neat, but a spacewalk? Maybe Leanne should have come instead. Carrie knew that Leanne was made for this kind of thing. Carrie instantly realized why she loved her friend so much.*

As they approached the space station, she saw a strange spaceship docked on the other side. It was red and yellow, and looked old and beaten, with strange markings she didn't recognize on the wings and tail. "Earth Shuttle regulated to docking station three," a voice said over the speaker.

"Shuttle bay three. Making changes on coordinates," Rafa replied, tapping his console.

The ship rose up, banked a hard right, and hung upside down. It made Carrie disoriented, and she had to close her eyes. The shuttle lined up alongside the docking platform, and huge magnets fit themselves against the ship, locking it into place. It reminded Carrie of being on a plane when it would taxi into the terminal. Except this was in space, which was much cooler.

Both Max and Rafa flipped switches above their heads and then raised their hands so as to not touch anything. Carrie watched as the console flashed with symbols and numbers.

Max glanced back, catching the worried look on her face. "There's nothing to worry about, Carrie, the space station has an automatic docking protocol. We just let the station do all the work," he said.

"What is that ship?" she asked, pointing to the one she had seen coming in.

"Oh, that's a Bogarian Ship from the Eagle Nebula. They are like the police of the universe," Max reassured her. "They look like warthogs and can be very brutal if you break a space law, but no need to worry. We are well within our galactic rights."

"So, aliens really do exist?" Carrie asked.

"Oh yes, far more than you can imagine. There are millions of aliens. We are aliens too, to every other race," he noted.

"But we're not aliens. We're from Earth." Carrie rubbed at her temples, trying to push away the building headache.

"Which is just one of billions of planets. Earth is just the one that still believes it's alone in the universe," Max said.

Carrie looked away. He was right. All this time, she thought they were alone in the universe, and therefore, all other species were aliens. But Earth is just another planet, and Earthlings are just aliens to everyone else. She smiled as she thought about all the different species that must be out there. "How many alien races have you met, Uncle Max?"

"Seven." He grinned back at her.

"Docking complete," the ship chirped. The ship rocked a little but then went still. Max, Rafa, and Carrie got up and headed back to the door. Rafa released the seal, letting in a loud hiss of air as the pressure equalized. On the other side of the door was Harry, a Bogarian. He was only about five feet tall, but thick with muscle. Max was right—he looked just like a warthog and wore cool armor and a helmet. He grunted, his large nostrils flaring. Then he laughed.

Max and Harry immediately embraced each other. The little alien picked Max up as though he didn't weigh a thing. "Maximilian! It has been far too long for us not to have seen each other! I have missed you, my friend."

"Harry, great to see you! Meet my niece, Carrie." Max reached back and pulled a wide-eyed Carrie forward.

"Niece?" Harry asked.

"My sister's child. We call them nieces for girls and nephews for boys," Max explained.

"Ah!" Harry said. "We have the same on Bogar. But we say chutee and nuntee."

"Hello, Mr. Harry." Carrie felt very shy and wanted to hide behind Max, but she gathered up her courage and smiled at the Bogarian.

"The pleasure is mine, niece of Maximilian. You shall be my chutee as well!" He pulled her in for a hug just like he had to Max. She stiffened, then relaxed, giggling. She was now considered a family member to an alien species! How cool was that!?

Harry moved on to Rafa next, exchanging more hugs. "Harry, you look as healthy as ever!" Rafa exclaimed.

"You flatter me. I am old and sore." Harry made a face.

"Oh, that's right. Your birthday was two months ago! I'm sorry I missed it," Rafa said as they walked into the station.

"Graah, you didn't miss anything. It was just a thousand of my in-laws, and Brathu's mother was in rare form. Just what I needed to bring in my 107th birthday."

"Did you say you are 107 years old?" Carrie didn't mean to interrupt, but she couldn't help it.

"Don't remind me." Harry grunted as he waved a security card in front of a pad, opening a sealed door.

"Is that old or young for a Bogarian?" Now that she had gotten past the surprise, she wanted to know everything.

"Well, I'm technically still young. My father is 1,100 years old."

"1,100?!" Carrie stopped dead in her tracks. The men all chuckled. Max gave her a nudge.

They walked through a large control room where a few different alien races were working on computers, along with several humans. The Bogarians, who guarded the doors and patrolled the hallways, were the only ones armed with weapons. Carrie saw a group of aliens that looked like goldfish. They seemed friendly and waved at her with their fish arms inside mechanical arms that gave them fingers. However, their heads were in space helmets that looked like giant fishbowls, complete with water. On the other side of the room, she saw a huge ten-foot alien that was holding up a large section of an engine. A humanoid female approached them with a holographic tablet that was projecting some sort of trajectory around a planet. Carrie stared at her face because she had glowing purple eyes and long white hair tied into a ponytail. Her skin was a lavender color and had scales.

"You are beautiful," Carrie said to her.

The female alien smiled wide, showing her white teeth. "Thank you."

They continued walking for a moment. "That was a Retelly. They are very similar to like a salamander. Very skilled fighters, scientists, and comics."

Carrie laughed. "Aliens do comedy?"

"Humans do comedy. Why can't other species on other planets also do comedy?" Uncle Max asked.

Carrie thought about for a moment. "I just never thought of the social interactions of an entire other species doing normal things like drinking coffee and cracking jokes," Carrie said.

"Well they do, and honestly, they are really funny."

They finally came to what looked like a large, empty airplane hangar, with helmets and air tanks on the wall. "This is the walk room," Max said as they approached the equipment.

Carrie watched Harry put a helmet on Max and connect the breathing tube to the apparatus on his back. Carrie could tell it was an oxygen tank. Each tube had a red and blue tip; the former attached to the belt and the latter attached to the oxygen tank. Then Harry spun a strange circular tube and a small thruster popped out on each side of Max's tank. "Remember how to use your jets?" he asked.

"Huh, you invented these things?" Max laughed, using both his thumbs to point at himself.

"Some fat Earthling did, if I recall correctly," Harry replied, making Rafa laugh.

"You call it fat; I call it love jiggles." Max did a little dance, making his gut move around.

Still laughing, Harry led Rafa out of the room. "Once they open these doors, we'd be sucked out."

Max attached a clamp to a metal ring on his belt. The clamp was connected to a cable and reel attached to the wall. He walked up to two glowing foot pads in the center of the room just as they filed out. There was a loud *Ku-Chunk* as the magnetic components reacted. Carrie and Rafa went into the observation room. They could see everything on a flat screen monitor the size of a truck. As they watched, the huge bay doors opened, and the blue lights on the foot pads turned green. Max leaped up like Superman. Carrie watched with wide eyes as her anxiety took over. She was both elated and completely afraid.

Max reached the end of the cable. He floated in space for a moment before unbuckling his clamp and using his thrusters to maneuver toward the large telescope. "Almost there," he said into his microphone.

"You're doing great," Harry replied encouragingly.

Carrie turned to see Harry sitting at a monitoring station. She walked over so she could see everything from Max's point of view. The telescope looked so much bigger this way. Max was getting closer when Carrie noticed something moving off to the left of the screen.

"Uncle Max, did you see that?" she asked.

"See what?"

"Something moved on the telescope."

Max looked around but didn't see anything. Suddenly, a laser beam shot past him, followed by several more. Max moved quickly, using his thrusters to spiral toward the telescope. He dodged more blasts.

"All units! Agent under attack! Unknown aggressors. All units respond. Human on spacewalk. Use caution." Harry yelled over the intercom.

Sirens started walling throughout the station, and several Bogarian police units moved quickly. They were outside the space station in seconds. Carrie watched about thirty of them jet into space with laser rifles ready. They leaped off the side of the space station like frogs while using their thruster packs to navigate toward the telescope.

CHAPTER 25

Leanne pushed the helicopter to its limits as she pulled it up and over the last copse of trees. She could see the military camp in the distance, and lights flickered against the frozen town. She looked at her TAC COM. She looked to the sky, wishing she could see what Max and Carrie were doing, but all she could see was a strange light show. "What do you think that's all about?"

Robbie moved up so he could see the red lights flashing. It looked almost like one light going back and forth, but Robbie knew better. He'd seen laser fights in his favorite movie, Robo-Police Ultra Ninja Force. He looked at Leanne with a lump in his throat. "It's not good."

"Then we need to get this job done and ASAP."

As they got closer, the console started to beep and red lights flashed. The monitor showed several incoming rockets. Leanne didn't say anything, but she reached up and pulled her seat belt latch tighter. Robbie sat back down and did the same.

She raised them higher into the sky before pushing a few buttons. A burst of fiery debris launched out from underneath the helicopter. She pulled the steering yoke hard to the right and the helicopter went almost completely sideways. After a tight horizontal turn, she pushed the joystick down hard. They plummeted toward the ground.

Robbie was busy working on his TAC COM. He placed a grappling hook in the end and programmed an algorithm. "Just get me over the alien missile, I'll do the rest."

"It's a hot zone, so I can't land. You'll have to grab it on the fly!" The helicopter leveled out over a small section of houses and flew past the neighborhood at top speed. Three helicopters missiles were still in hot pursuit.

"I don't need you to land. I do need your TAC COM, though," he shouted.

"What? Why?"

"Just give it to me."

Leanne quickly pushed a button on the bottom of her TAC COM, releasing it from her wrist. She felt weird not having it on. She hasn't taken it off in two years. She handed it to Robbie. "You break that, and I'll kill you!"

"Yeah, yeah." Robbie put her communicator on his other hand, loading it with a grappling hook as well.

"What are you going to do?" Leanne asked as she pushed the joystick all the way to the left. The helicopter tipped on its side again. A rocket went sailing underneath them.

"I have an idea. Just get me close."

Robbie made his way to the gunner seat and leaned far out of the helicopter. Everything slowed down as he watched a rocket burn past them with only inches to spare. But he had to focus on that alien sphere missile sitting in the frozen field.

Leanne pulled the joystick to the right, making the helicopter turn wide. "I'll circle around and fly straight up from the ballfield," she shouted back to him.

Robbie waited until they were in a range. He had no idea what he was going to do, but he knew he had to get that UFO into the ruby box, no matter what. As they shot past the baseball field, he got an idea. "Get low to the ground. I'm going to water ski!"

Leanne glanced back. "What? Really?"

He nodded.

"You got it. You know that if you hit any of those frozen soldiers you're going to splat like spaghetti, right?" she asked.

"Oh yeah, if that happens, I'm toast. I won't hit them."

Leanne dropped the helicopter to just ten feet off the ground. Robbie stepped out onto the landing rail while holding onto the inside of the helicopter. He leaned out, getting ready. "Wanna slow it down a little?"

"I did. We're only going 150 knots," she hollered back.

"Oh, well then," he rubbed a hand across his face. "Here goes nothing!" Robbie leaped out, raising his left arm toward the helicopter. He fired the TAC COM, and the cable spiraled out with a whizzing sound. The grappling hook slammed into the helicopter's side. Robbie dangled behind the helicopter just off the ground. He tried to gently touch his feet to the ice, but the speed nearly jettisoned him into the helicopter's spinning blade. He reeled himself in a little and tried again. His feet tapped the ice, and he bounced again, but not as high. He looked down to see a rocket shoot past him and explode into the ground. "What is wrong with these idiots?!"

Robbie dropped again, putting his feet to the ice one more time, and this time it worked. He was skiing behind the helicopter.

"We are three hundred yards out from the object!" Leanne said over the microphone inside his helmet.

Robbie reeled in the cable a little, but bullets started peppering the ice in front him. *Great, now I have to dodge bullets too.*

Leanne looked at the button for the machine gun but didn't want to push it. She would feel really bad if anyone was hurt because of her. Except, they were being pushed to the limit with rockets, and now machine guns, being fired at them. She looked out to see Robbie skiing across the ice and dodging bullets. She didn't know what to do. They were in over their heads. They were literally about to open fire on the military.

Then she saw another helicopter engaging the others. "I'm going to clear you a path!" Commander Collins said over the mic. "You get to the object! I've got your back, Team Adventure Club!"

Leanne watched as two helicopters exploded. She slowed them down a little, and Robbie released the cable. Now he was on his own. He skated down the ice at a hundred miles an hour. He bent his knees and leaned forward, focused on his objective. He could see it now. He shot the grappling hook into the ice and used it to slow him down a little. He dropped to his side and slid feet first at it. Pulling the box from his pocket, he released the grappling hook and let it reel itself back into his TAC COM. He slid to the UFO with the box out and open, capturing the object inside. As he skidded on his butt, he slammed the lid shut tight.

Leanne looked down to see the missile, but it was gone. Robbie had done it! She cheered before realizing he was still going. She knew he wasn't going to stop unless he hit something, so she had to catch him. She sped up and was just about to reach him when the console alerted her to another incoming missile.

She had to move quickly. She pushed the joystick down and to the left. The helicopter dove straight down, almost spinning completely on its nose toward the frozen ground. The rocket hit the ground behind her and exploded, damaging the tail rotors. The helicopter lifted up and was immediately out of control. It spun wildly, heading right for Robbie.

Robbie immediately thought the worst. As the helicopter spun past him, he could see Leanne desperately trying to steer it. With his right hand, he shot his TAC COM at the frozen ground and aimed his left at the helicopter. He waited for the right moment and fired. The grappling hook shot through the air and right at Leanne. She saw it coming and unsnapped her seat belt, moving for the passenger area right behind her seat. The doors on either side of the helicopter were open. The wind was wiping hard, and the helicopter only had seconds before it was out of control completely.

She swiped the screen on her TAC COM, finding her own grappling hook and firing it at Robbie's hook. The hooks smashed together, interlocking. Leanne jumped out of the helicopter just as she and Robbie pressed the retract buttons. She whipped to Robbie as Robbie was pulled to her, both of their TAC COMs operating at full capacity. They met in midair, slamming into each other. Leanne was able to do a somersault upon landing.

Robbie, however, was jerked from the ground, wiped across the ice, and sliding wildly.

Carrie landed perfectly. The helicopter spun recklessly, crashing and exploding behind her. She watched as Robbie shot past and as he did, he tossed the box in her direction. "Take it!"

The box slid to Leanne, and she scooped it up. She put it in her pocket just as Commander Collins landed in front of her. The whirling propellers shuddered to a stop as he climbed out of his helicopter and saluted her. "Good job, soldier!"

Robbie slid on the icy terrain, trying to slow down. He managed to roll to his back then brought up his TAC COM, pressing the retract button. The grappling hook shot back to him and into its place on the TAC COM. He then fired it again into the icy ground. He stopped almost immediately.

"Thanks for saving my life," Carrie said, grinning at him.

Robbie laid on his back exhausted and out of breath. He breathed a sigh of relief. Everyone looked over to him as he gave a thumbs up.

"I'm good!" he yelled.

CHAPTER 26

Max was using part of the telescope for cover. The lasers slammed into it, each blast melting it a little more. "Any clue as to who is attacking us?" Harry's voice crackled inside Max's helmet.

"The same ones responsible for the freeze missile-UFO-thingie on Earth. The Orthonians. They want our planet to become a frozen tundra so they can take over," Max said, leaning out and firing his TAC-COM laser at them. He hit one of the Orthonians, sending it spinning out into space.

Carrie watched on the monitor as the battle continued. "Uncle Max, be careful!"

Max made his way around the telescope, landing on a flat surface. He magnetized his boots and ran to meet up with two Bogarians who were returning fire. He stuck his hand out, and one of them tossed a laser rifle to him. He held it for a moment. Even though it had been a lifetime ago, the weight was familiar; he knew this weapon well.

He was sick of fighting. So much violence and death across the entire universe and all over the same thing. Someone else's stuff. Planet, water, food, money: it was always the same. He took a deep breath, flipped a switch on the rifle to automatic, watched the light meter fill up, and got ready.

Max pushed off the telescope with both feet. He needed a better vantage point. He fired, hitting an Orthonian before coming under major fire again. He kicked off a support beam, magnetized himself on another platform, and ducked behind cover. The solar panels started to move into a secure position as to not take any more damage. As the panels turned, Max could see the reflections of several of the Orthonians waiting for an ambush.

"We have five minutes, Max. I just got word from Earth. They have isolated the missile, and it is secure," Rafa said.

"I'm pinned down!" Max shouted.

Max saw an air pressure hose just above the group of Orthonians shooting it. The hose burst shooting freezing air at the aliens. One of them got their entire right arm frozen.

Carrie didn't hesitate. She ran back to the jump room, and quickly put on a helmet, oxygen tank, and thruster pack. She ran to the foot launch pads, and they lit up as she stepped into position. "Launching in five, four, three, two, one," the computer said in its emotionless voice.

Rafa looked at Harry. "What's launching in airlock?" He accessed the security feed and gasped. Rafa ran to the bay door, but it was too late. The room had already been pressurized, and he couldn't stop it. "Carrie! No!" he shouted, banging on the window. He watched helplessly as she launched into space without a secure cable.

Carrie hurtled out into the cold expanse of space at full speed. She had her hands down by her sides, gripping her thrusters. She looked at the telescope and the warring Bogarians and Orthonians. She navigated through some debris when she was hit by a piece of broken solar panel. She slammed into a large piece of metal, knocking her head hard. She was dazed for a moment. Suddenly, there was a white flash on the inside of her eyelids. As she opened her eyes, she could see her trajectory laid out before her. It was all there, like a heads-up display on a GPS. She just had to follow the path. Robbie's mistake with the glasses was paying off. With the aid of the calculations, she maneuvered through seemingly impossible openings. Her first objective was to take out the Orthonians. She floated past a Bogarian. "Toss me a rifle!"

The Bogarian flung his weapon at her, and she turned back around, flying sideways. She lined up her gun and shot an Orthonian in the foot, knocking him off the telescope. This freed up Max who was able to start moving up to the lens. Carrie circled the platform, knocking Orthonians off one at a time while avoiding every attempt to take her out.

Max reached the top of the telescope where an Orthonian was waiting. It aimed its gun at Max. "Give up, Earth hero!"

"Never." Max smacked the gun out of the small alien's hand. He slammed its head against a metal rung, knocking it out, then stuffed it into a small alcove for retrieval later. He used his access card to open the door to the lens controls.

"Two minutes, Max!" Rafa shouted.

Max was inside the telescope now. It was small and cramped. He opened a console and entered the coordinates to Bellevue Heights. The telescope rotated away from the sun and toward Earth. He continued to input the commands, ignoring the warnings stating that what he was doing was considered dangerous. He heard Carrie land nearby and fend off more aliens, but he had to stay focused.

"Forty-five seconds, Max."

The Bogarians made their move and apprehended the few remaining Orthonians taking them into custody.

Max entered the last few numbers and the telescope aligned with the sun. A beam of light shot through the telescope, lighting up the inside. The word "SUCCESSFUL" blinked on the monitor. Carrie and Max laughed and hugged each other.

They could hear the whole space station clapping through their headphones. "C'mon, let's get back," Max said.

Leanne and Commander Collins were still standing in the field when a wave of warm sunlight washed over them. They basked in the warmth. Leanne grinned. "They did it!"

Commander Collins tilted his head, questioningly.

"Carrie and Uncle Max. They went to space to align the YOLO Telescope so that the sun could melt the town," she explained.

"That's ... really?"

"Yeah. That's the kind of stuff we do," she beamed proudly.

"You mean besides flying military-grade helicopters and having dogfights?"

"Well, that too. But mostly we save the day."

"We?" Commander Collins asked.

"Yeah, Team Adventure Club!"

"Team Adventure Club? I like it!" He gave her a salute, grinning as the ice laden grass beneath their feet started to melt.

Leanne rushed over to Robbie who was still laying on the ice. She laid down next to him putting her head on his shoulder. "You're not too shabby, Robbie."

"And you're not a bad pilot." He leaned over and planted a kiss on her cheek.

Leanne turned pink. She looked away, bashful, and saw two military men walking toward them. She recognized Secret Inspector Bonnefield.

"Leanne, I trust you have the box in safe custody?" he asked.

"Well technically, it's a ruby container," she said. She nodded, fishing it out of her pocket and handing it over.

"Amazing job, kids! I am more than proud of you."

"No matter what you do, never open it," Leanne warned.

He chuckled but nodded. "You don't have to worry about that!"

"What a night!" Robbie said.

"I just want to go to bed," Leanne said, letting out a breath.

A dark shadow covered them as they laid there on the ice. It was a huge space of some kind. Leanne and Robbie didn't move as the thruster kicked up snow and wind around them.

They laid back in the mud and watched as two figures jumped out of a ship. Leanne helped to steady Robbie as they got to their feet, and then they rushed over to where the others landed. "You guys did it!"

"Us?! You managed to get the UFO into the ruby box!" Max scooped them all up in big hugs.

"That was all Robbie!" Leanne bounced on her toes.

"Me!? You took out thirty helicopters. You should have seen it!" Robbie shouted.

"We fought aliens in a laser fight!" Carrie was practically vibrating.

"Aliens?" Robbie's eyes went wide.

"Yeah, like *real* aliens. I met like ten different species. Max's friend looked like a warthog! He was named Harry. The others were scary—they wanted to take over the Earth!"

"I'm just glad you're safe!" Leanne hugged her best friend hard.

"So, who wants to do it again?" Max asked.

They all looked in different directions, avoiding eye contact before cracking up.

As the sun rose for the day, the telescope heated the ice, thawing out the town and sending icy cold water rushing toward the beach. Everyone was confused and wet.

Malcom, Robbie's best friend, was still sitting at his computer staring at his homework. He jumped when the ice thawed him, and his electronics came back to life. His computer sparked and the screen black. "What? No. No. No. My homework!" he wailed. Then he looked around and saw that everything in his room was soaked. "Wait, why is everything all wet?"

Poor Miss Tinderam's dog finally made it back home. She was cold, shivering, and quite damp. Miss Tinderam found her poor little girl on the front porch and picked it up, squeezing it so hard it looked as though its eyes were going to burst right out of its head. The dog just licked her in return.

Sadly, no one will ever know what happened that night. No one remembered, and not a soul will ever discover that Team Adventure Club saved their seaside town. Everyone will just go about their business as usual: going to work, going to school, having fun at the beach, and playing in the parks. The world isn't ready for people like Carrie, Leanne, Robbie, and Uncle Max. They are a new breed of hero. They are the few who have no fear when faced with danger. They are the ones who fight monsters, robots, and the bad guys.

They are Team Adventure Club!

END

AUTHOR BIO

Joe Davison's work spans twenty-five years of writing, directing, and acting—and can be seen in the Netflix smash-hit *Stranger Things* ... where he stars as Nerdy Tech in Season 2.

He has written over thirty-eight screenplays and 7 novels: *Cold Front, Zoey Saves Christmas, Infinite Chaos, Death's Campaign, Shindy Shine, The not so True Adventures of Sam and William*, and the supernatural crime noir series, Mike Strong.

Joe Davison has also directed 6 feature films, including *Experiment 7, As Night Falls, Frost Bite, Mr. Engagement, Beauty is Skin Deep,* and *Sorority of the Damned*.

More books from
4 Horsemen Publications

Young Adult Fantasy

Blaise Ramsay
Through The Black Mirror
The City of Nightmares
The Astral Tower
The Lost Book of the Old Blood
Shadow of the Dark Witch
Chamber of the Dead God

Shattered Start: Story of Sera
Sins of The Father: Story of Silas
Honorable Darkness: Story of
Hex and Snip
A Love Lost: Story of Radnar

Joe Davison
Cold Front

C.R. Rice
Denial
Anger
Bargaining
Depression
Acceptance
Broken Beginnings:
Story of Thane

Valerie Willis
Rebirth
Judgment
Death

Middle Grade

J.B. Moonstar
Russ and The Hidden Voice
Taylor and the Red Wolf Rescue
Jenna and the Legend of the
White Wolf
Jenna and the Eyes of Fire

Jan and the Secret Cave
Jan and the Search for Lilya
Taylor and the Final Nine
Michelle and the
Missing Manatee

Discover more at
4HorsemenPublications.com